A Second Chance

Barry Mink M.D.

Barry D. Mink M.D.
1122 Medicine Bow Rd.
Aspen, Colorado 81611
970-923-5988
barrymink@comcast.net

Registration Number TXu1-735-222

ISBN: 0615609201
ISBN 13: 9780615609201

"The god I believe in is the god of second chances."
Bill Clinton

"Baseball is ninety percent mental. The other half is physical."
Yogi Berra

"The future isn't what it used to be."
Yogi Berra

This is the story of a young man who was a tremendous athlete in high school. He signed a professional baseball contract and was expected to be a major-league ballplayer by all who saw him play. However, early in his career, misfortune occurs, and he has to give up baseball. Fate gives him a second chance to play baseball again, this time at the major-league level. Through the genius he acquired in sports medicine, he is able to make a remarkable comeback that changes the way baseball and other sports will be played. It gives all of us who love sports hope for a second chance.

Prologue

Dr. Ben David knew that it had worked. All those years of preparation, trial and error, had now paid off. He felt remarkably good after running for nineteen hours and logging ninety-nine miles at the Leadville hundred-mile trail race.

It was just before dawn, and the headlamp he had been using to stay oriented to the trail and his nocturnal surroundings was no longer needed. He had crested the power line hill after an hour of running uphill. Running downhill now was a relief after so many hours. The last mile was ahead of him, and although tired, dirty, and caked with dried sweat, he had a feeling of exuberance that was more than emotional. It was physical as well.

The enzyme cartridge that was attached to the angiocath in the cephalic vein of his upper arm had worked perfectly. It supplied the oxidative enzyme at just the right intervals and proportions so that muscle glycolysis was not impaired under such demanding circumstances. Ben knew that at this point of the race, muscle damage was so profound that the enzyme CPK produced by injured or overused muscle would be in the many thousand range, while normal CPK at rest is only about one hundred. The enzyme he had worked on for the last several years along with his unique energy polymer drink was now perfected. The enzyme allowed muscle work to continue at high levels of performance, even after several hours of running the tough high country terrain of Leadville, Colorado. He knew his CPK would not be in the thousands and he was going to finish the race with a very good time.

Ben now approached Main Street, the final pathway to the finish. A few curious onlookers were on their porches and gave solitary cheers as he passed. There was no nausea, no muscle pain or cramps, and no excessive fatigue.

The race organizers and a few town officials were holding a red, white, and blue finish tape in the surreal light of dawn. There was no fanfare, cameras, or news reporters to commemorate this fantastic endurance achievement. Ben thought this simple recognition of such a major breakthrough in sports performance was quite ironic. He crossed the line with a smile that most thought was a grimace, but in reality was bemusement. Dr. Ben David was sixty-five years old, and he was excited about what lay ahead.

Chapter 1

The David household was at a high level of anticipation. Eli David was nervous. He constantly was taking out his white handkerchief to blow his nose, a lifelong trait, when situations like this were happening. He was a muscular and compact man that had watched his son excel in sport, far exceeding his own abilities.

Eli was a former all-American soccer player in college and spent three years playing professional basketball as a guard for the Rochester Royals. His career never took hold, and he spent the ensuing years as a physical education teacher in the Chicago school system. His son was now on the verge of a professional sport career. In just a few minutes, the Cincinnati Reds regional scout was about to visit and discuss a professional baseball contract for his son Ben.

Ben had just finished high school and was already planning to go to college and play football for Ohio State on a full scholarship. He had been heavily scouted after winning a league championship and being selected all-state quarterback. He had several offers and had been the guest of several universities. Chartered jets, fancy hotels and restaurants, as well as alumni hospitality parties were all part of the routine to enhance interest in the school. However, after many family discussions, Ohio State had been select- ed by his father for their outstanding athletic program un- der famed coach Woody Hayes. The winning tradition of this coach and his uncompromising attitude about success is what appealed to Eli. Woody always worked his teams hard and was tough on and off the field. "The only loser is a good loser" is a familiar Woody quote. His mother wanted Ben to go to Northwestern for its academic reputation. It also meant having her son closer to home. Dad won out, and Ohio State was chosen.

At this time of year, the baseball season had just ended, and another state title was won, with Benny again lead- ing the league in batting, slugging percentage, and home runs. Every major league scout in the Chicago area had made offers, but Cincinnati had made the best preliminary offer, and they had the inside track. All that was left was to hear the final offer and sign.

When the doorbell rang, Sarah David already had hot corned beef sandwiches made and cold beer set out. Eli opened the door and greeted the overweight scout. Frank Cogan was still panting after climbing up to the second landing. Temporarily out of breath, he still shook Eli's hand vigorously in his desire to be friendly and make a good first impression. Eli led him into the living room, introduced him to Sarah and Ben, and offered him a seat.

"We are very interested in having you with us and being a Cincinnati Red," said Cogan after regaining his breath. He got right to the point, which impressed Eli. This man did not bother himself with nuances. "I am prepared to offer Ben a bonus of twenty-five thousand dollars to sign, six hun- dred dollars a month with fully paid expenses while on the road, and to pay you, Mr. David, a salary of two hundred dollars a month as a scout for the Cincinnati Reds."

Eli had difficulty controlling his excitement since this was much better than he had anticipated. "Please have some lunch, Mr. Cogan," he said as Sarah handed the sandwiches over.

"Thank you," said Cogan as he reached for one, then fumbled trying to hold on to the thick, oozing sandwich while eyeing and reaching for the cold bottle of Schlitz at the same time.

Cogan felt more relaxed now after having gotten the offer on the table right away, observing that Eli David had the look he had recognized over the years as that of a man who had swallowed the bait. The corned beef and cold beer went down well as Cogan looked over at Benny. He recognized the boy's muscular resemblance to his dad, but he was taller and more graceful in his movements. His dark eyes were serious in their stare, and his manner was friendly and confident. He was quiet, with an inner intensity that came through as a very positive trait to the learned eye of Cogan.

"That's very generous, and we are certainly happy to hear this," said Eli, letting his enthusiasm reveal itself.

Ben had been asked what he thought, but he was content to see his father so happy with the new prospect of being a recognized scout and the financial relief that they could now enjoy.

Cogan had opened the battered briefcase that he carried with him and took out a group of papers. He was careful not to let the mustard and juice of his sandwich contaminate them. "Look over these documents and sign so we can get Ben out to Geneva and join the A club before July fourth. The team is on a pennant run and in dire need of help," said Cogan with a broad smile.

Eli and Ben gathered around Cogan, oblivious to what the stern and puzzled face of Sarah David was about to reveal. The celebratory atmosphere had an interruption. The question came loud and clear from Ben's mom. "What about his college education?"

Ben was the first to turn around and see his mother's face. Cogan and Eli took a moment before confronting that familiar stare Eli knew all too well. No compromise would be accepted. Over the next sixty minutes, the men offered several rationalizations that Sarah would not buy.

"This will mean so much for your son and your husband. The money can buy anything the boy needs. We expect him to be a major league star in no time. Your husband will have a new career."

None of these arguments caused her to change her mind.

"I see we have a problem," said Cogan dejectedly.

Eli knew Sarah was right. His son, who had always done well in school, had to have a college education as a back-up. Just as he had experienced with his own college education, one could not count on athletics as the sole support of his son's future. "My son has a plan to play football for Ohio State, and that comes with a guarantee of a full college education. I agree with my wife, and we cannot accept your offer, but thank you for your generosity and confidence you have in my son."

Frank Cogan realized he was not going to get a deal today. "I can't believe you would throw this deal away," he said, surprised. He had never gotten this far with a deal like this and left without a contract. He stood up and went for the door in a manner that was quite different than his jovial entrance.

Sarah said good-bye cordially, and Ben said good-bye with a puzzled and ambivalent tone. Eli accompanied Cogan out on the landing.

"Mr. Cogan, my son has greater potential to be a great baseball player than football player. My wife doesn't realize these things, but I do. His education needs to be the first priority, I know that, but he has an extraordinary inner ability that words can't explain. It's what great athletes have. He understands what it means and takes to win. I have rarely seen it in my career, but I know he has it. It will be a waste not to give him a chance."

"I understand and agree, Mr. David, and you have not heard the last from me. I will see what I can do." Cogan turned, and descended the stairs faster than he did when he first came up. He knew he had to talk to the front office and check a few things, but this kid was too good a ball-player to let go and play football.

Chapter 2

The drive along Lake Michigan passed some beautiful old houses that occupied the very old, wealthy communities of the near north side. The Tudor-style mansions with expansive front lawns and weathered gates stood tired and bored amongst the century-old elms and maples that protected them. Ben David didn't notice these old guardians as his father drove and talked with newfound energy.

The call from Cogan had come just in time to stop the argument over baseball or football. Sarah could not be swayed, and Eli just couldn't accept the fact that baseball could be taken out of his son's future. He knew his wife was right, for the right reasons, but his emotion could not be just shut off for what he felt was in his son's best interest.

"Mr. David, we are prepared to stay with our original offer, but we will also get your son into Northwestern to start the fall term after the season with the Geneva Reds, all expenses paid."

There was a moment of silence for the news from Cogan to sink in. The silence did not reflect the joyous explosion going on inside of Eli David.

"There will be a few preliminaries, but these can be arranged over the next few days," said Cogan with authority.

It didn't take but a few hours for Sarah and Eli to agree, and Benny knew his future was now going to be behind the plate, wearing the "tools of ignorance." Ben was a catcher with one of the strongest arms the scouts had ever seen. The arm was what made him stand out from all the others, even though his hitting and swing were major-league material. His throw to second was a laser, sometimes even from the squatting position. It truly was breathtaking. Eli remembered during one game when the runner tried to steal second. He was so far from the bag when the throw arrived that he stopped dead in his tracks in the middle of the base path in total amazement, shaking his head as the shortstop ran over to him to make the tag.

The turn off Lake Shore brought the '56' Chevy onto the main drag of the Northwestern campus. Deering Library loomed across the vast meadow on the right as Eli looked for the turn into the Department of Education parking lot. Not many students were around since it was early summer and summer classes hadn't started yet. It was easy for Eli to park the Chevy next to Dean Summer's parking space and walk only a few paces to the office entrance.

As Eli and Benny entered the old Gothic building, there was a line of students talking and laughing while they waited for the registrar secretary to open her desk. Eli quietly approached the woman at the reception area, who looked up with a brief smile and asked if she could help them. They were fifteen minutes early, and she asked them to wait in one of the well-worn red chairs while she let the dean know they were there. They were alone as they sat down, and Eli spoke in a very hushed voice.

"You will now find out what clout really is, my boy, even in these ivory-tower places."

Northwestern had a year waiting list for students, even for the 3.5 grade-point students who went through the long application process. To be able to get into the school at this late date was unheard of in normal circles. The obvious "favor" was apparently in play here.

"The dean will see you now, please," said the smiling secretary, and Eli and Benny followed her into the spacious, book-lined office of the dean.

The desk was large, oak, and dark. The thin, bald-headed man behind it was almost hidden from the view that Eli and Ben had when asked to sit down in front of it. The atmosphere was formal and stuffy, exactly what one would expect being in this setting.

The dean spoke first, using a soft, slow voice. "So you want to be a teacher, Mr. David?"

Ben hesitated for an instant, thinking that maybe the dean was speaking to his father.

"Uh, yes, sir," Benny finally said.

"Very well, see the secretary at the registrar desk, and she will have you fill out the necessary papers. Good luck, young man." The dean stood up, walked to the door, fiddled with the knob, and seemed to have difficulty with the pull to open it. He acted as one in a hurry to get on to other matters as he showed the pair out without another word or handshake. Ben and his father walked out into the hallway, somewhat dazed by the brief, comical protocol.

"Mr. David, please," a plump, rounded women with glasses on a chain called out from behind the desk. She stood up and waved the Davids up to her, ahead of the line of students, who stopped their talking and laughing. Their smiles changed to suspicious looks of disdain as the two walked through their gauntlet.

She led them to an alcove for them to complete the application forms in private. It did not take long to fill them out, as many of the sections were blocked out in red marker. These were the areas of grade point average, school awards, and teacher recommendations. Ben then had his picture taken, and an ID card was issued that recognized Benny David as a freshman in the new arriving class.

It was very anticlimactic. The thrill that was supposed to be felt for entering one of the most prestigious universities was replaced by a very uneasy disappointment. The two didn't talk about it on the quiet ride home.

Chapter 3

There was a small celebration at the David apartment sending the young man off on his new journey. Friends and family hugged, kissed, shook hands, and smothered Benny with their congratulations. Most of the older relatives were impressed with his entrance into Northwestern, but the younger friends were excited about the prospect of knowing a future major leaguer.

"Don't forget I want tickets whenever I want."

"Can I have an autograph?"

"Will you send me a bat?"

"Can you get me the official ball, or a team hat?" were the common jokes that Ben had to smile and respond to. It was realized by all that Benny David was a celebrity with a future beyond them all.

The next morning, after his mother made his favorite breakfast of waffles and bacon, he loaded his two large duffels into the Chevy and slowly walked back into the kitchen to hug his mother for their first good-bye. They both cried, she for understanding that this must be, and he because he loved her.

His father drove him to O'Hare to catch the late morning flight to Rochester. There was no crying when they said good-bye, but his father's hug was firm and uncomfortable in lasting longer than Ben had anticipated. His father was his idol, and he was his father's pride.

The Greyhound bus arrived at the Kirkwood Hotel at 6:00 p.m. The ride from Rochester to Geneva introduced Benny to the pastoral Finger Lake region of central New York. Sleep was not an option as the bus made its way through hills,valleys,and lakes that had the charming traditional appearances described in history books. The uniqueness of the terrain was quite a change from the familiar flatness of the Midwest,

The Kirkwood Hotel had a fresh coat of white and green paint, but it reminded Ben of an old woman trying to look younger by dyeing her hair and wearing heavy makeup. Ben entered carrying his duffels and approached the main desk, which was unattended. Looking around, Ben noticed down the hallway a banner with red lettering announcing: Geneva Redlegs. He walked over to find the office empty, most likely because of the late hour. Walking back to the desk, he found an elderly white- haired man sitting there at the desk, yelling into the phone. He hung up and looked angrily at Ben. He waited for Ben to talk first.

"I am the new catcher for the Redlegs and was told to report here," said Ben with a smile.

The white-haired man cussed through an alcoholic breath indicating his displeasure at having to deal with a late check-in. A key was given with brief directions to the second floor and his room, 202. There was no request for Ben to fill out any registration and no offer to provide any other help. Ben felt intimidated by this welcome and meekly picked up his duffels, and walked up the squeaking, worn staircase to his room.

The door opened without the key, revealing a very stark room. The floor sloped more than thirty degrees, and the single window overlooking the street had a vertical crack that was easily noticed because there was no curtain or shade. There was a single bed, a single card chair, a paper-board dresser, and an old, stained sink against the middle wall. There was a radiator that was clinking, a single towel, and a used bar of soap. There was no closet, but a hat rack to hang things on. Ben sat on the bed, sinking six inches into the mattress. The pillow had an unusual smell that Ben had trouble identifying.

Too tired to go out and find something to eat, Ben slowly changed into his sweats and grabbed the towel and soap. He walked down the hall to the bathroom to relieve himself and check out the shower. After closing and locking the door, Ben stripped and got into the brown-stained stall and waited for the weak stream of the shower to get stronger. It never did. Getting the soap off took some time, and the water started to lose its warmth, prompting Ben to get out and wipe off the residual soap that remained.

Walking back to his room, Ben met no one. Getting into the awful bed, Benny felt sad and lonely. He already missed home. He dressed and went downstairs, wanting to find the phone and give his parents a call to tell them he had arrived okay, and to hear their voices. The phone was on the front desk, and Ben picked it up, only to find no dial tone. It was dead.

The white-haired man came out of the back angry and yelling. Ben thought he was going to come over the desk and start hitting him with the broom handle he was carrying. "The phone cannot be used after six, so get the hell out of here, you bastard!"

Ben backed off and turned up the stairs to his room. He was shaken, lonely, and very tired. However, sleep did not come until well after midnight. This introduction to professional baseball was not what he had expected.

Chapter 4

The late morning sun came in obliquely through the cracked window, awakening a disrupted sleep. As Benny awoke, turning over on the very soft mattress, he confronted a strange couple standing next to his bed. A man with a nose that looked like the inside of a pomegranate and a woman who was almost bald, missing her front teeth.

"Better get your ass out of bed, son. It's well after breakfast," said the man with an impatient but friendly tone.

"What time is it?" said Benny, still not quite awake yet.

"It's ten o'clock, and we are here to clean the room."

Benny realized he had overslept. He tried to jump abruptly out of the deep softness of the bed, but was unsuccessful, falling back and springing in double pump fashion before being able to get up. A little embarrassed and standing in front of the two, he could see that they were enjoying this by the jolly smiles on their distorted faces.

"No worries, dear, this is your first day, and we know you had a late arrival," she said in a motherly tone.

Benny relaxed and felt more comfortable in their presence. "I am the new catcher for the Redlegs," he said, hoping to impress them.

"Oh, we know. I am Joe, and this here is Molly. We tend to all the ballplayers who stay here. You're the only one staying here right now."

After finally getting them to leave, Benny quickly got dressed and left for the Redleg office downstairs. He liked the old couple, but realized there was not much of a calling to clean the rooms of the Kirkwood. They were friendly enough, and the threat of that initial introduction seemed to dissolve.

Reno DeAngelo was sitting with his feet up on the desk, reading the *Geneva* Times, when Benny opened the door. The office was furnished with two rows of folding chairs and a green felt card table with scattered cards and chips covering its worn surface. A large blackboard was mounted over the desk, with the starting lineup chalked in from yesterday's game.

Reno looked over his shoulder and smiled with the whitest teeth Benny had ever seen. "You the new catcher?" he asked, as Ben shook his head yes.

"I am one of the starters, throw lefty, and am leading the club with a sixteen and two. My slider is hard to handle. It falls off fast. Counting on you to handle it."

Benny walked over and held out his hand. "I am Benny David, pleased to meet you."

The handsome pitcher stood up, revealing a large frame and long arms with hands almost touching his knees. "Pleased to meet you, rookie." He squeezed Benny's hand, overlapping it easily. "Riley had me wait for you, but the rest of the team is already out at Shuron with morning batting practice. I am supposed to take you out there as soon as you got here."

Ben apologized for oversleeping, which didn't seem to get a response from Reno.

"I guess you haven't had breakfast yet, so we will stop on the way," said Reno as he led him to his red Corvette parked just outside the door.

16

Reno was only one year older than Benny and came from Luray, Virginia. He had the usual stardom in high school, being the winningest pitcher the state had ever seen. He signed a big bonus, bought the Corvette, and played last year for Palatka in the Florida State League. He learned how to control his fastball and slider that year, but not after taking his lumps with ten losses. Control was his problem, and he still needed more of it, but this year he'd modified his right foot placement, which seemed to help.

He filled in Ben on the routine and schedule of daily activities as Benny tried to eat his breakfast quickly. Reno liked Ben on first impression, but he was doubtful that a rookie would have what it takes to take over as catcher. Reno wanted to win twenty this season and win the pennant. They were four games behind the first-place Auburn Yankees with one month left to go. His usual catcher, Lopez, was a veteran and knew the opposing hitters. He was adequate behind the plate, but not major-league material, and he was only hitting .200. Reno was anxious to test out this new catcher as soon as possible.

The ride was quick to Shuron Park, being only six blocks from the hotel. They arrived as the team was coming off the field after working on hitting and going through some infield practice. Reno led Benny into the clubhouse, which was under the right field stands. Ben stood there self-consciously as players walked by him into the lockers and showers.

"Hey skipper, here is the new guy," Reno said as Harry Riley walked up.

"Hi, kid, welcome, I manage this gang," Riley said in a whiskey voice as he shook Benny's hand.

"Hey, listen up, everyone. This here is Benny David. He just got in and is a catcher. Show him the ropes."

Ben was uncomfortably aware of all the stares. Some were friendly enough, while others seemed indifferent.

"Listen, kid," said Riley, "we are short on unis, so Reno here will get you what we have."

Ben followed Reno into a back room where uniforms were hanging on a heating pipe surrounded by bats, catching gear, and the floor cluttered with all types of old baseball equipment.

"You're not going to like this, but our gray traveling uniforms are all gone, so we only have these older unis that the team used to wear a few years ago," said Reno with a grin.

The uniform was made of a gray silk material that was not the traditional gray flannel that most ballplayers were used to. It looked very strange and felt even stranger when Benny tried it on. It felt like he was wearing some article of clothing that a woman would wear or be accustomed to. It also was a bit tight in the butt, making Ben feel even more self-conscious.

When Reno gave him the white home uniform to try, Ben was relieved to see it was the same as what the rest of the team was wearing. When he tried it on, he realized it was way too big. The legs came far below his knees, so the red stockings barely showed.

"It's all we have," said Reno, seeing Benny's disappointment.

Ben stored all his gear in the locker that Reno showed him. It was next to Lopez, the current catcher.

Lopez was from Havana and spoke little English. He was older and appeared stern. He didn't look very healthy, with a yellow tint to his eyes and pockmarks on his cheeks, and he was almost bald. Ben tried to strike up a friendly conversation, but gave up after Lopez glared and ignored him. Lopez started to speak Spanish to some of the other Hispanic players near him and walked away.

Chapter 5

The old yellow school bus, known as "the Greenbriar" for reasons unknown, pulled away from the Kirkwood on what was to be Ben's first road trip in professional baseball. The bus was crowded and noisy, as the team was on its way to play the Corning Red Sox later that evening. Reno was the starting pitcher and made it a point to sit next to Benny.

"Riley said you're going to start as catcher tonight, and I wanted to go over some of their lineup."

Ben listened very attentively as Reno went on and on about how he was going to pitch, naming everyone on the Red Sox team. The drive seemed to go very quickly, as Ben's nervousness kept him from tiring of Reno's rambling. The GreenBriar finally arrived in Corning two hours before game time, allowing batting and infield practice to take place.

Ben dressed in the tight gray silk uniform he had been given. His teammates didn't help his embarrassment by howling and making fun of the rookie.

"Hey sweetie, you forgot to powder your nose tonight."

"Be sure to smile for the boys out there."

"Where are the pink shoes?" being just of few of the taunts that Ben had to put up with. It didn't stop with his teammates, for as soon as Ben went out on the field for infield practice, the stands erupted into continual harassment, dishing out much of the same. It was relentless.

Benny had never been exposed to this kind of punishment, spending his high school games in the limelight of being the favorite on the field. In high school, fans never gave him jeers. Even the visiting stands would applaud in awe at his accomplishments.

Ben couldn't hide these new feelings, even behind the catcher's mask he wore. His embarrassment led to anger, causing him to look over his shoulder at the stands—a big mistake.

"Hey kid, don't make it worse by acknowledging it. Don't be a rabbit ears!"

This came from Ozzie Jenks, the very large black umpire standing behind Benny calling the game. Ozzie took no shit from anyone and didn't go out of his way to help any player. But he, too, was getting irritated by the constant attention Benny was getting from the stands and had to help the rookie out. Ben put his mind back on the handling of his pitcher and quickly learned a basic rule: shut out the crowd.

Reno had a fastball that moved in very well, and his slider was a real dropper. Ben had no trouble catching either one and was impressed with Reno's abilities. Ben soon shut off the crowd with a demonstration of throwing two out trying to steal, and picking one off of first with a shot from his cannon arm. All were impressed with the rookie, as the Redlegs went on to win seven to three, and Reno won his seventeenth game of the season.

Ben had no real problems hitting the opposing pitcher's best stuff, going two for three and walking once. It was as if the ill-fitting silk uniform had taken on a new meaning for all concerned.

At game's end, after Reno retired the side, Ben jogged out slowly to the mound to congratulate him. "Nice job, Reno" he said in a matter-of-fact tone, but Reno gave his catcher an unexpected hug that lifted him off the ground as if he were a feather. Reno realized this was going to be a battery mate who was the real deal.

The ride back to Geneva was raucous and happy as the team celebrated the victory. Benny was getting most of the attention even though Reno was the star.

Flaco Hernandez, the shortstop, gave Ben a hearty pat on the back with the most genuine show of joy, shouting, "*Bueno, bueno,* Beenny!"

Harry Riley sat up front grinning behind his chewed cigar, knowing the team now had a big chance for a league championship.

It was late before Ben got back to his room at the Kirkwood. The old desk clerk was there as Benny went for the phone to call his folks. He was excited to tell his mom and dad about his first professional game. As Ben picked up the phone, the old man aggressively approached, yelling and screaming that it was too late to use the phone. In reaction to the attack, Benny jumped over the desk counter, knocking the broom handle the old man was reaching for onto the ground. He grabbed the man by the front of his shirt and, with a very powerful grip, lifted him off the ground and sat him down with a force that startled both of them. The old man's face went pale, and his eyes started tearing up. Benny didn't have to say anything. His actions and expression caused a fear in the old man that could be identified only by the old man's inability to respond except in a garbled muttering.

Ben released his grasp and turned slowly to the phone and dialed up the number. The old desk clerk didn't move as Benny delivered his good news and completed the call. His father was ecstatic and questioned his son about the game specifics. His mom just wanted to talk about his room and food, but Benny exaggerated his description of the situation so as not to worry her.

When Ben finished, he turned back to face the clerk, apologizing. "Sorry to have to do that, but this was a very important call."

The old man shook his head, nodding in agreement, as he watched Benny go up the stairs to his room.

Chapter 6

The Geneva Redlegs continued to play winning baseball with Benny behind the plate. The last series of the season was to finish in Auburn, with the Yankees and Redlegs tied for first. The winner of this final game would be the league champs.

The Greenbriar pulled into Auburn Field two hours early not only to get in a good batting practice, but also to avoid the harsh treatment that was anticipated from the Auburn fans. Auburn was a blue-collar town that was home to the state penitentiary and a very large brewery. It was also very close to Geneva, about an hour drive, which also contributed to the intense rivalry between the two teams. Auburn's population consisted mainly of hardworking families of Polish and Slavic extraction who loved their team, beer, and sausage in that order. They would never pass up the chance to abuse the opposing team.

Riley stepped off the bus first and was immediately greeted by fans yelling obscenities and throwing used popcorn and peanut boxes. Ducking, the Redlegs ran to the clubhouse very surprised by the early appearance and intensity of the drunken crowd.

It didn't get any better as the Redlegs took the field for batting practice. Auburn Field opened several hours before the opening pitch. The stands were packed to full capacity four hours before game time, and the beer tent was also open as the first fans entered the field. The odor of Polish sausage, beer, and sauerkraut was overwhelming, but not as overwhelming as the catcalls, boos, and swearing that were continuous for the several hours before game time. The crowd was well tanked, impatient for the game to begin, and loving it all, knowing the advantage it would have for their Yankees. The more noise and abuse they could dish out, the better.

Benny warmed up Reno, liking the movement of his slider and fastball. Reno was more nervous than usual knowing a win would mean twenty wins for the season and a league championship.

"You feeling loose and ready?" said Riley as he walked over.

"Feeling good, no worries," said Reno, and Ben confirmed to Riley that Reno was on with good stuff.

"Play ball!" yelled Ozzie Jenks as Flaco walked up to the plate to face the first pitch.

The game was well played by both sides, and even zero to zero going into the ninth. Reno was still in there, pitching a two-hitter, while Auburn switched in a new pitcher in the eighth. He was their closer and could throw harder than anyone else in the league. He was usually unhittable, but that would only last for a few innings before he tired.

Ben came up with two outs and nobody on. The stands were throbbing, and the noise was deafening.

"You can hit this guy. Just relax, kid," said Riley as Benny walked to the batter's box.

Ben took his stance and had a good feeling. It seemed his neuromuscular system was very ready, but calm. It was like the feeling an athlete gets on rare occasion, when

24

everything seems to line up. The brain relaying confidence to the rest of the body that all is perfect for the task at hand, referred to as "being in the zone." No subjective hesitation, all involuntary reaction as the body does what it wants without any control or supervision needed from the higher brain centers. It is a "done deal," and the signal, although surreal, is interpreted by the athlete as something very strong.

During the windup, Benny was very still, calmly waiting as the ball was released from a very powerful motion by the big right-hander. There was no hesitation as the eyes coordinated the torso. The arms and feet pivoted with the right timing and power to meet the little sphere as it was a millisecond in front of the plate. The fine feeling as the sweet spot contacted the pitch made it no doubt to Ben that the hit was solid. It became no doubt to those present that this was going far over the fence.

The crowd was never so quiet that day as Benny trotted around the bases. The only noise one heard was his teammates jumping and screaming, jumping on the young catcher as he touched home plate. Ben was grinning ear to ear, catching a look at the big right-hander, who stood in disgust with hands on hips and a face reddened by the shock of it all.

The last half of the ninth still had to finish, with the Yankees power hitters coming up. Reno had trouble with the first two hitters, both getting on base with a walk and single. The next batter was retired with a strikeout, but the next batter walked. The bases were loaded with one out.

The crowd was into it now, cheering in a way that was more like praying and chanting with nervous enthusiasm. Tension was very high.

The next hitter stepped up and swung at the first pitch, hitting a hard grounder to Flaco at short. He was playing a bit back for the double play, but changed his mind by throwing the ball right at Ben, who was stepping on home for the force. Ben took the throw and fired to first for the double play and the end of the game.

The runner coming in from third, however, didn't appreciate that the game was over and hurled into Ben with full force well after the ball was thrown to first. Ben went flying, not expecting the impact. He was stunned and instinctively got up to charge the runner, who collided with him. Both benches started to empty, and the crowd was going nuts. Benny's charge was quickly interrupted by a sudden sharp pain to the angle of his jaw. His consciousness changed from rage to daze as he fell to the ground, very surprised, before having a brief period of unconsciousness.

Ozzie Jenks immediately delivered a strong right-hand cross directly to the chin of Benny, dropping him before he could engage the Red Sox runner. Ozzie then picked up Ben and ran with him to the dugout as the crowd started to leave the stands and pour onto the field. The players from both sides engaged in brief combat. The Auburn police, who were used to riots at Auburn Field, were prepared, rushing the field and stopping a serious riot.

Benny awoke in the clubhouse with the big smile of Reno looking down on him. He felt nausea and had some blurred vision, but it was only a few minutes before he realized where he was and what had happened.

"Old Ozzie probably saved you from major hurt by that sucker punch," said Reno, still grinning. "The crowd was about to maul you on the spot if you had been allowed to get into it with that runner. Come on. Get up. No shower, we have got to get out if here pronto."

Reno and Flaco helped Benny to the Greenbriar as police surrounded the bus. Dazed, Ben got into the bus amongst loud, continual cussing and threats from the unhappy crowd. It took only a minute for Greenbriar to speed away into the cool night, away from the chaos of Auburn, and on to the tranquility of Geneva. High school baseball had never been like this.

Chapter 7

Lefty's Bar was the center of social activity in Geneva. It had been a tavern for over a hundred years and was now owned by Lefty Vennata for the past forty. It had sawdust and peanut shells on the old wood floor, and the smell of beer was permanent. The long mahogany bar was old and original, as were the white globe light fixtures that looked like burned marshmallows from all the years of accumulated dust and debris.

Lefty was behind the bar and pulling on the draft handle with his remaining left arm, his right had been amputated above the elbow. He was laughing and talking loudly with Riley who was hunched over at the bar nodding his head and smiling while nursing a beer.

The team was celebrating their win and championship. Ben was over at one of the dark booths with Reno and Flaco drinking Lefty's free beer while other teammates were in groups loudly talking and laughing as well. "Pizza's will be out of the oven soon, everyone drink up" yelled Lefty not missing a chew on the dark cigar hanging from his mouth.

Riley came over to the booth were Ben, Reno, and Flaco were camped. "We couldn't have done it without you guys, you are the backbone of this team. Congratulations on a great season! I'm proud to have been your manager" said Riley emotionally.

The three men looked down embarrassingly and muttered brief acknowledgement. Riley knew this was going to be his last season as a manager. He was getting ready to retire to Florida this winter.

The pizzas came and the men jumped up gladly to end the conversation and get their share when Riley grabbed Benny by the arm. "Sit down kid I want to tell you something." Ben sat back down next to Riley as Reno and Flaco left for the pizza table. "I have managed and been in baseball a long time son, and have seen some of the greats. You, in this short period of time you've spent in pro ball, have demonstrated some amazing talent. You have what it takes to be right up there with the great ones. I don't say this lightly. You have the passion for winning that is stronger than I have ever seen. This counts more than talent. I am serious about this! I wanted to tell you this because I won't be around baseball anymore. I am going to retire and become a spectator. When you are up there winning ball games and breaking records I want you to remember that old Riley was the first to recognize this. You and Reno have a great future in baseball and I hope I am around long enough to see it." Benny looked him in the eyes and clearly saw his sincerity.

"Thanks, Coach, I appreciate this. I have learned a lot from you and the team. I will try to make you proud." They shook hands, and Ben went over to join Reno and Flaco, who were already eating pizza and drinking beer.

"Well, college boy, you going to get so smart you won't talk to us next year," said Flaco with his mouthful of pizza. They all knew Ben was off to Northwestern in a few weeks to start college.

Reno also chimed in with, "All those rich, pretty college girls to choose from may be a bit dangerous for a young boy like you."

Ben smiled, loving the kidding, knowing it as a form of acceptance by his mates. "I'll miss you goofs. Not many at Northwestern to remind me of the lower forms of society."

The three men were really enjoying each other's ribbing and having great fun celebrating the fantastic success they had had. This was interrupted as all three turned their heads simultaneously when Lopez, the old catcher, approached their table.

"*Lo siento mucho,*" the older man said in a quiet voice.

"He is very sorry," said Flaco to interpret.

Lopez extended his hand to Ben and actually had a smile on his weathered face. Ben took it as Flaco interpreted Lopez's words.

"You have my respect, young sir. You play baseball very well, and your arm is the best I have seen. You will go far in baseball. We will play again together, my friend."

The sincerity of Lopez was very powerful. A long silence followed that was finally broken as Flaco and Reno offered Lopez a beer. Ben toasted them all as the best young team in baseball.

This was not an exaggeration. Baseball experts would all agree with this observation. There would be discussions for years in the New York- Penn League back rooms and bars that this was truly the best team that ever played for Geneva, New York.

It was several beers and hours later that the group finally got to bed.

Chapter 8

Todd Worthington was at his desk looking over the pledge list of freshman who would be coming through the Sigma Alpha house next week. Sigma Alpha was the fraternity house that looked like a country club lodge in the middle of the Northwestern campus. The house had elaborate stonework and large pillars that resembled the finest mansions of the North Shore. Slate roof, oxidized blue-green gutters and drainpipes framed the ivy-encrusted walls, while crystal stained glass windows peeped through the massive fields of foliage. It was a temple founded to house the well-bred, wealthy, good-looking, and especially the stars of the athletic fields, then, now, and in the years to come.

Sigma Alpha always had a very aggressive rush policy to get the best recruits of the incoming freshman class who fit this privileged mold. Todd Worthington was the rush chairman, whose duty it was to get this accomplished. The Sigma Alphas would stop at nothing that money could buy to have the best. They put on the best parties, dated the prettiest women, and kept a code of conduct that promoted egotistical exclusivity from the lower-strata students of Northwestern University.

The upcoming "rush week" was where the freshman class spent the week visiting the fraternities on campus. Through a process of social interaction, meeting the active members of the various fraternities, a mutual decision would be made by the fraternity and the freshmen to pledge and join the fraternity. The Sigma Alphas took this process very seriously to get the pledges they wanted for their fraternity.

Benny David's name was at the top of the list Worthington was studying. "We've got to go see this kid before rush week starts so we get the inside track," he said to his roommate, who was sitting across his large, polished oak desk.

"It's against the interfraternity rules, and we can't risk the penalties again for breaking them," said the roommate.

"Bullshit, this kid will be worth it. He is a real jock, and this fraternity can't afford to lose him to another rival," said Worthington, almost shouting. "You and I will take a drive into Chicago and see him this weekend."

Worthington loved these tough challenges, having no doubt he could win over Ben David and his family quite easily. Who could resist what Sigma Alpha had to offer?

Chapter 9

It was good to be home. Ben could smell the familiar odor coming from the kitchen as his mom cooked dinner. His mom loved to cook for her son and see him enjoy her simple but homemade food.

"Tomorrow some guys are coming to talk to me about joining their fraternity," said Benny to his dad as they sat in the well-lived-in living room that was always the scene for family discussions.

"Good, I was a Tau Ep at Illinois. Although I had to wait on tables for my room and board, it was worth it to be part of the fraternity. We were comrades sharing the college experience above and beyond the classroom or athletic field. We lived in the same house, eating, sleeping, and studying together. We matured and grew up together, having a bond that lasts to this day. I made lifelong friendships in my fraternity that I continue to have and cherish. It was a major part of my college education, getting along together." Eli continued to encourage his son about the benefits of a fraternity experience as they were called to dinner.

A SECOND CHANCE

It was late morning when Todd Worthington and his roommate walked up the stairs to the landing and rang the doorbell. The two wore blue blazers with the Sigma Alpha crest embroidered on the front pocket. Repp tie, white starched shirt, gray slacks, and polished brown cordovan shoes rounded off their outfits.

Ben opened the door wearing his Levi's and high school sweatshirt. "C'mon in, guys," was all Ben said as he led them into the living room, where his mom and dad stood up from the worn upholstered couch and greeted the college boys.

After cordial introductions were made, Worthington went into his sales pitch, without trying to show his excitement too much, about the prospect of having this young star ballplayer join Sigma Alpha.

His enthusiasm, however, could not be contained as he dominated the conversation, going on and on about how proud they would be to have Ben join them. There were even references to having his room and board taken care of for the first year, or longer, if he was able to help them win the intramural football championship that was so coveted and won every year by Sigma Alpha.

Ben just smiled as he took it all in and was actually impressed with all the attributes Worthington outlined.

Worthington could feel the impression was a good one as Ben's mom brought out some chocolate brownies and milk.

"You know, Todd, I was a Tau Ep at Illinois and want Benny to join a fraternity like I did," said Eli as the boys helped themselves to the brownies.

The shock on Todd Worthington's face was immediate. Ben didn't recognize it, but his dad sure did. Eli knew the kind of fraternity Sigma Alpha was, and he didn't approve. He wasn't surprised as he watched Todd Worthington's face redden and his eyes dilate in disbelief at the news. Tau Ep was a Jewish fraternity, and there was no way in hell that a Jew would be allowed into Sigma Alpha, no matter how good an athlete he was. Eli was saddened to have to bring this up like this, but he had to be sure that he was not mistaken. His impression was confirmed by the change in attitude of Todd Worthington. He suddenly became introverted and uncomfortable. He squirmed as he tried to think of a way to retract all he had said, but to no avail.

He finally stood up and in a shaky voice, uncharacteristic for him, stated the lateness of the morning and that they had many more freshman to see. They abruptly started for the door, and Ben had to almost run to get to the door and let them out.

Eli didn't say much as the door closed.

"They seemed like nice guys," said Ben, but his father just turned and went into the kitchen to join his wife. He knew his son would have to find out the hard way what he had learned years ago. Some things never changed, and he hoped his son would handle this in the right way.

Worthington cussed as he drove out of the alley car park. He should have known. The name, the neighborhood, the chocolate brownies, it all was so obvious. "We'll have to make it bad for this kid when he comes over during rush week. You know the usual plan for the geeks."

The roommate just nodded as they sped away in the immaculate Austin-Healey 3000.

Chapter 10

It was a beautiful, crisp fall day along the lakefront campus of Northwestern, with the maples and elms giving full colors of red, yellow, and orange. Benny walked along fraternity row trying to find the Sigma Alpha house. Excited freshmen were everywhere, dressed in their finest corduroy and wool sweaters, rushing to get to the designated fraternity on time.

Ben had no difficulty finding the Sigma Alpha house since it was the largest and most austere on the row. The old, magnificent stonework was typical of the mansions of that era, and the walls were covered with old-growth vines that the season had turned to a golden reddish brown. The roof was gabled and the windows leaded glass. A large mahogany door was garnished with old, heavy hardware that had turned a greenish gray with time.

The door opened surprisingly easily for being so large, and Ben entered a large foyer that was surrounded by trophy cases filled with athletic awards commemorating the achievements of the Sigma Alpha athletes. The foyer was crowded, but a large, muscular fellow came right up to Ben and introduced himself.

"Hi, I'm Scott," he said with a big smile. He extended his large hand, and Ben took it.

"I'm Ben David, glad to meet you."

The big man lost his smile and looked a bit puzzled, but regained his jovial composure in a few seconds. "Ah, Ben, we have been expecting you. Follow me."

Scott led Ben through the crowded main living room to a side room that was used as a TV and card room. Six freshmen sat and stood around talking quietly with each other. There was a pitcher of apple juice on a card table, with some American cheese and crackers set out as well. The atmosphere was quite a contrast to the loud party-like atmosphere in the main room that Ben had just walked through. In the main room, there were fancy sandwiches on a long table and kegs of beer in every corner. The laughter was loud, as everyone in this room was having a great time.

Scott walked Ben over to a large, overweight man who was talking to a small-statured, but fit-looking Asian man. "This is Ben David," said Scott as he quickly turned and anxiously left the group to join the main party.

"Hi, Ben, I'm Bob Lincoln. Friends call me Pudge," said the big man. He weighed about 280 pounds, had a big belly, but his upper body, shoulders, and arms were massive and strong. "This here is Denny Luh."

Denny warmly smiled and shook Ben's hand firmly.

"It's obvious we are considered lower-class citizens. These bastards have segregated us out 'cause they don't want to deal with us. I'm fat and Jewish, he's Asian and what are you? You don't look Hispanic," said Lincoln angrily.

Ben was dumbfounded at the situation. He had only rarely faced prejudice, and never to this degree.

"Shit, let's get out of here," said Lincoln as he started to push toward the door.

As he was moving away, a tall, very thin black man approached the group. "Hey guys, what's happening?" he said with a big, mischievous smile and friendly gesture.

Lincoln stopped in his tracks, turned, and faced the happy man. "Are you a Sig Alph?" he fired out.

"Hell no, man, I'm one of the geeks, like you."

They all laughed, and even Lincoln smiled. The ice was broken, and the group of labeled misfits started to find out more about each other.

Denny Luh was from Hawaii and had been all-conference wingback for his high school football team. Lincoln was an all-city Chicago tackle, and Clay Stevens was an all-state basketball forward for his Indiana high school. Athletics was a common bond for the group, which caused the hour to go by very quickly as they joked around and drank the apple juice. When it became time for them to leave, they left together as a group, laughing and walking by the Sigma Alphs standing in the foyer.

Ben saw Todd Worthington, who was among them, trying to hide from his notice. Ben just smiled. What started out bad had turned out okay. Ben had made some good friends and found out that Sigma Alpha had something rotten inside that beautiful house.

The group broke up to go to other fraternity houses that were on their schedules for that day. Ben had the Phi Tau house as his next appointment and followed the fraternity row path all the way to the far quarters of the quadrangle. Hidden behind two large oak trees was the Phi Tau house.

It was a half duplex that had been built in the 1940s to house GIs at the end of World War II who were on the GI Bill. It was constructed of wood and mason blocks and was not kept up well. The roof slanted, and the front windows and door needed some paint badly.

Ben entered the foyer, which was small and had no trophies. The floor was very worn linoleum, with a crude inlay of the Phi Tau coat of arms.

He was greeted by Art Cohen, a hefty fellow with clear, penetrating dark eyes and a great laugh. Smiling broadly, Art came over with a very cheerful welcome and introduced himself in a strong New York accent.

"Hello, welcome to Phi Tau. I'm Art and am glad you're here." He then escorted Ben into a very simply furnished living room much smaller than the one at Sigma Alpha.

Benny liked Art immediately, mainly because of his friendly nature and ability to make him feel at home. He was introduced to several other members of the fraternity, and none of them looked very athletic. They were all friendly and seemed loose and casual, again making Ben feel very comfortable and at home.

Art took Ben aside, and the two talked for several minutes. "Our fraternity has several advantages for you to consider. We are always number one in scholastics, with our grade point average higher than any other house. We have the winner of the Big Ten debate championship and several members of the debate team here as well. We are known for our artistic accomplishments in theater, music, and art. Are you musically inclined?"

Ben chuckled and said no. His interests were athletic. Art gave his big smile and stated simply that they had no real top athletes in the house, but there was always interest among the fraters to be spectators. Art went on to explain that he himself had played softball in Central Park and loved football. He admitted he knew about Ben's baseball prowess and his signing with the Cincinnati Reds. This information about the incoming freshmen who would be participating in rush week had been distributed to all the fraternities.

Ben and Art walked over to the beer keg that was tapped in the living room. Standing amongst the group at the keg was the very large Bob Lincoln.

"Hey Ben, long time no see," said Lincoln amusingly. "This is a little different than the Sig Alph house, eh! More of my kind of people. Plus, most of the guys here are Jewish. We should get our buddies Clay and Denny to get over here and see this place. What do ya think?"

Ben didn't answer right away, being a little embarrassed with Art standing there.

"Come on, Ben, let me show you around the rest of the house," said Art.

On the tour, Ben could see the physical nature of the place was well below the standard of the rest of the fraternity houses. But, the members were happy, friendly, and going out of their way to introduce themselves and talk.

A few hours later, Art had Ben come to his room so they could talk privately. He was president of Phi Tau and therefore had the largest room in the house. Ben made himself comfortable in a large, well-worn leather chair, and Art sat behind his desk. Art wanted Ben David to be a Phi Tau mostly because they had never had a super athlete in the fraternity, but also because, over the last few hours, he realized Ben had other attributes not seen commonly in super athletes. He was modest, spoke intelligently and softly, was polite and respectful, just an overall nice guy,

"We would like you to be a member here," said Art simply."

Ben stated that he had reservations and expressed his concerns about the emphasis that Phi Tau placed on non-athletic endeavors. Art was prepared for this conversation and pointed out that Ben could change the emphasis. More importantly, the fraternity could open new outlooks and experiences for him that a "jock house" would not offer. Literature, art, music, appreciation of the finer things in life, and being with people who had different backgrounds and interests would help broaden his horizons.

Ben knew Art was right. He had not been exposed to these "finer" appreciations and was quite interested in experiencing them. He liked the people he met here and realized it could be the right thing to do. He also knew his father would be happier with him joining a predominantly Jewish fraternity.

"I'll let you know in a few days, and thanks for the offer."

Art accepted the decision and cheerfully led Ben out where, surprisingly, there stood Denny and Clay, who were due to visit the Phi Tau house next.

Chapter 11

The first few weeks of classes were over, and the quarter was in full swing. Ben had not been very stimulated by the Department of Education curriculum. Sociology, speech for teachers, and organizing a class lesson were examples of the subject matter that did not appeal to him. However, he knew he was going to be a pro ballplayer and he just had to endure this first quarter. Besides, he enjoyed walking on the beautiful campus.

The education school had the prettiest girls, which made the dull classes seem bearable. He also had started exercising every afternoon at the university's fully equipped gym. It felt good to be active again after the long fall lay-off. Weights, jogging, and throwing a football with Clay and Denny kept him happy.

Clay Stevens, Denny Luh, and Bob Lincoln all joined Phi Tau. Ben David did too, liking the friendly and casual atmosphere of the house. Art Cohen's influence had also played a big role. Ben found it to be true that exposure to people with non athletic interests would be a valuable experience.

Ben wasted no time in organizing an intramural football team to compete in the eight-week season that was just about to start. Intramural football was the most popular fraternity activity in the fall, and all the houses took it seriously, especially the Sigma Alpha house, which made it a priority.

The game allowed blocking, but no tackling. The ball was dead after two hands touched below the waist. There were six men on a team. A center, two receivers, two blocking backs, and a quarterback. Clay, who was tall and had good hands, and Denny, who was very fast and shifty, were chosen as the receivers. Big Bob Lincoln, or Pudge, was a blocking black, and Art was hefty and fast enough to be the center. They needed another blocking back, which was a challenge for the fraternity since nobody wanted to risk doing it.

The Phi Tau fraters were curious about the whole idea of having a football team. Interest was there, but it was not a priority. The team practiced every afternoon, but there were no spectators from the fraternity, only the five players led by Ben, who called the plays and was quarterback.

It didn't take long for the team to get in sync, especially with the accuracy and strength of Ben's arm. His passes never missed, and both his receivers had no problem hanging on to the accurate throw. They all were having a good time and realized that, as a team, they were good together.

"What are we going to do about another blocking back? Our first game is in five days," Ben asked Art after a long practice that went into the early darkness of dusk.

"I have an idea that I will present to the fraters at dinner tonight," Art said as they finished practice and walked back to the house.

The fraters all ate together in a large dining room that was in the basement of the house. Freshman waiters served in white jackets. Otherwise, there was no formality, but the food was good.

Cohen tapped his glass to get attention after the blessing was said. He stood up before the group with a serious demeanor. "The Phi Taus have a new identity to establish. We have a group of freshmen that have organized a football team. I have joined them and want others to join them so we can be represented in the league for the first time in our history. It is a chance to show we can be more than a bunch of scholars, musicians, and actors. It will expand our experiences and horizons. We need at least two more players, especially one that can play blocking back."

There was a brief silence, followed by a few nervous laughs. A few of the fraters did speak up and thought the idea of a football team was hilarious.

"We will be laughed off the field and humiliated, let alone killed by those big jock houses. They will love to beat the shit out of us."

The group agreed, and nervous laughter continued with increasing crescendo in defense of the idea that the fraternity would be made to look like fools. During this commotion, Ned Kowalski stood up, and the room immediately became quiet. Kowalski never had much to say, so it was a surprise to all that he made this effort.

Ned Kowalski was big and very muscular, having grown up on a farm in Wisconsin. His priority, however, was getting top grades and being number one in his engineering classes at the tech school. Physics, mathematics, and calculus were the things he was interested in, not sports. He stayed in his room and studied, coming out only to eat, go to class, and sometimes ride his bike around campus. He was always very intense and had very little time for small talk or humor.

He slowly started to speak with a scowl on his face. "I will volunteer for this position of blocking back. I do not plan to be made a fool of." He sat down and casually started to finish his dessert.

The group was shocked and silent until Art stood up, thanked Ned for volunteering, and flashed a smile to Ben across the table. At least Kowalski was strong. It only had to be determined if he was coordinated enough to block and protect his quarterback.

Chapter 12

Saturday morning came bright and cool to the north shore of Lake Michigan. It was the first test for the Phi Tau football team. They were to play Alpha Omega, a smaller jock house that was never in the first division, but took their football seriously.

After breakfast, only a few Phi Taus came out to the field, while the Alpha Omegas had the entire house out to watch and cheer for their team. This bothered Art, who was in a bad mood and very disappointed in the poor turnout.

The team warmed up gingerly, but Art did not say anything. The Phi Taus had practiced together a handful of times and did have some basic plays that Ben had set up. They were enthusiastic, but Kowalski and Lincoln, the blocking backs, were slow. Cohen had some clumsiness in catching the hard throw. Stevens was fast and tall, but he never was serious about the whole thing. Denny was good. He could move quickly and had great hands, catching anything Ben could throw at him. Ben knew they just needed some time together and experience playing.

The game started with Alpha Omega moving down the field for a touchdown in eight plays. Lincoln was slow in rushing their quarterback, and Kowalski, kept running directly into their blocking back rather than trying to finesse him. The three-hundred-pound Alpha Omega back just had to stand there as Kowalski kept bouncing off. The few Phi Taus who were there held back the "I told you so" moans and started to think of excuses to leave and not be painfully embarrassed.

When the Phi Taus got their turn on offense, Ben astonished all who were there. Denny got free all the time, and Ben delivered the ball with speed and accuracy. A touchdown was made in fewer than five plays.

The Phi Tau sidelines went crazy, amazed that their fraternity could score at all, let alone so quickly. The smiles on the Alpha Taus changed to a more concerned look, but their expectation that this was a fluke was reinforced in their minds by the fact that, after all, these were the Phi Tau geeks.

The game continued, with the score close for the first half. This totally surprised both sides. Gradually, more and more of the Phi Taus made their way to the field as word got out that their team was scoring touchdowns. The half ended, and the score was tied.

The buzz that the Phi Taus were playing football and actually scoring could not be believed. Ben walked over to Ned Kowalski and tried to convince him not to just keep running straight ahead into the big blocking back. Ned always wanted to do things the hard way and loved the physical confrontation. He really didn't care so much for the score; he just wanted to continually punish the man in front of him. Ben tried, but couldn't convince him as the second half started.

The game stayed close, and the frustration of the Alpha Omegas increased. The crowds increased as the Phi Taus kept scoring. The Phi Tau sidelines were joyfully cheering, unbelieving their team's remarkable performance. The

Alpha Omega sideline cheered in a more hostile manner, unbelieving that their team was not running away with this.

The score was tied with only a minute left. The ball was only fifteen yards from a score for the Alpha Omega team. Kowalski still didn't change his approach in rushing, and their quarterback had too much time to throw the ball. Time-out was called, and the Phi Taus huddled around Ben.

"We are going to change our rush," he said. "Art is going to fake dropping back in coverage, and then he will rush the quarterback while Ned keeps banging away as he has been doing. This will leave the middle open, but either Denny or I will be ready for a pass in this zone." They all understood as the huddle broke up.

The next play, the Alpha Omega quarterback dropped back, confident he would have the time to hit his receiver in the end zone. He never expected Art Cohen to come barreling in from the center untouched. He tried to compensate by throwing quickly and off-balance. Denny was on the ball immediately, intercepting, but only advancing the ball ten yards. It was Phi Tau's ball with over seventy yards for a score and less than a minute left to play.

After three plays, the Phi Taus had advanced the ball only ten yards after Denny dropped one and a defender knocked one down. The third play, a rusher broke by Lincoln and sacked Ben behind the line of scrimmage. Last play to be called as the Phi Tau's huddled.

Ben called a play where Denny would be the supposed obvious target as Clay faked a slip and then ran as fast as he could to the end zone. Ben hoped Clay's height advantage would be the difference.

"Give me enough time, Pudge, so Clay can get to the end zone," said Ben as they broke the huddle.

The anticipation on both sidelines resulted in tense silence as the play was called. Ben had to move out of the pocket as the Alpha Omegas' rushers came with newfound speed and intensity. On the run, Ben calmly saw Clay had fooled his defender and was two steps ahead on his way to the end zone. Ben did not have any more time as he threw a high, arched seventy-yard pass to the spot in the end zone that anticipated Clay's position. Clay jumped high, but was unable to grab the ball in a catch. He deflected it upward, and out of nowhere, Art, who was always quick to follow a play, caught it just before it hit the ground. Touchdown!

The crowd now had grown considerably, and the noise made at the catch was like an explosion. Clay, Denny, Pudge, and even Ned jumped all over Art in uncontrolled enthusiasm. Ben felt himself being lifted up by his fellow Phi Taus and carried over to the pile of his screaming team-mates. The Phi Taus were out of control with happiness. This was never expected, so the shock of it all was electrifying.

After the initial celebration died down, Alpha Omega's captain came over and shook hands with Ben. "Congrats, you guys surprised us. Your offense was awesome. Good luck the rest of the season."

Ben thanked him and knew the Phi Taus now would have some respect.

The Phi Taus trailed off the field and walked the short mile to their house singing their fraternity songs and laughing. It was a very good feeling to win, a feeling that Ben had known before, but now fraters who lived in the realm of scholastics had had their first taste of athletic conquest. They could get used to this.

Chapter 13

The Phi Tau house had never seen so much excitement. All other interests and priorities took a backseat to the football team and their win. The house was animated, noisy, and popular. When the second game was to be played, several thought that now the "fluke" win would be shown up as luck. However, the team demolished their opponent by three touchdowns, leaving no doubt that they were for real.

The team won their next five divisional games, giving them the eligibility for the play-offs. Ben had instituted a stronger set of plays that were more sophisticated and diverse. Ned had learned to be a smarter rusher, realizing that the team could win without his brawn. He could use his brain and brawn together for a better outcome. Pudge lost a bit of weight by following an aerobic program that Ben had outlined for him. He was quicker on his feet and able to move better in his blocking patterns. He also felt much better, had more energy, and could sleep and study better. Clay had a height and jump that usually had him on the winning end of an alley-oop throw, and Denny could always get open with his speed and agility.

Art was ecstatic seeing how his fraternity was now functioning. The team was undefeated in its first season, getting the recognition from other fraternities that they were more than just a scholastic and drama house. The big test now would be the play-offs. Phi Tau had been playing in the weakest division. They were a small house that had no history of football success. They now had to play the second division champion in the first round of play-off action.

Delta Omega was a jock house and had the second best reputation for winning football games. They would always make the final play-off championship against Sigma Alpha, but never could get the final championship win. Sigma Alpha just had too much talent and always played a rougher type of game with their big blockers and rushers. Ben and the Phi Tau team knew this next game would be a tough one. If they could, by some miracle, defeat the Delta Omegas, they would have the opportunity to play in the all-intramural championship game. Sigma Alpha had already won and was waiting to see who it would face for the championship.

Todd Worthington, the captain and quarterback for Sigma Alpha, was finding it hard to understand and accept the success of the Phi Taus. However, he had the extreme confidence that they couldn't stand up to the strong Delta Omega team and that his team would face their usual opponent in the championship.

When the news came to Todd, he was eating his scrambled eggs and Canadian bacon in the elegant dining room of Sigma Alpha. He always enjoyed his breakfast because he compared himself in this situation to the lord of a very rich manor who expected to be served.

"The damn Phi Taus did it! They beat Delta Omega by a touchdown!" came the cry of the small crowd that charged into the dining room and destroyed the righteous elegance of Todd's special Sunday breakfast. The anger, disbelief, and finally the fear this provoked was almost unbearable for him. He spit out pieces of egg and bacon as he yelled to the astonished group that practice would take up the whole day today, and the Phi Taus would be shown the strongest and harshest tactics that Sigma Alpha could deliver.

Todd Worthington did not enjoy any of the time he had to spend before the championship game. He could not endure the fact that he and his superior fraternity had to deal at the same level with a group like the Phi Taus.

Chapter 14

The Phi Tau house vibrated with nervous tension on game day morning. Art Cohen did not have the familiarity with championship football games that Ben David did. This created a feeling of insecurity he rarely experienced, and it made Art agitated. When the team met before going out to take pre-game warm-ups, Art could hardly talk without his voice shaking. This never happened during national debate championships.

Ben was calm, as was Denny, reflecting their prior athletic experiences. Clay had lost his usual pre-game jocularity, looking more serious than any had ever seen him. Kowalski was the same before every game, stoic and quiet, wanting to get on with it and accepting whatever happened, happened.

Lincoln was boisterous and confident, perhaps hiding some of his anxiety. He had to face some very strong boys. He would rant out loud how he had scores to settle with those pompous anti-Semites, but most of the team just ignored his outbursts. The tension decreased a bit once all were on the field and warm-up drills started up.

The field was packed with onlookers from all fraternities and sororities. This was big. Ben hadn't seen this much enthusiasm at any of his past games, and it started to make him a little nervous too.

The Sigma Alphas had tremendous cheering sections and chants that thundered across the campus. The Phi Taus had a little band of brass players that sounded out fight songs, which accompanied the throng of shouts and yells, but not on caliber with the loudness and masculine vigor of the Sigma Alphas.

The game started and continued with high intensity. Both sides were nervous and jacked up. There was hard hitting by both sides, but the Sigma Alphas did not have the looseness required to time their throws with successful catches. They were "out of sync," a condition seen commonly when a team is too intense. On the other hand, the Phi Taus seemed more relaxed and focused. Ben had trained them very well, so they had no doubt what each play demanded. More importantly, Ben's confidence and performance on the field fired up his teammates to rise to a higher level of performance than their opponent.

Denny could get open quickly, making the short pass indefensible, while Clay gave them fits with his speed so that double coverage needed to be done frequently to prevent the long one. Kowalski and Lincoln held their own. They played the rough style that Sigma Alpha liked to play. They were not intimidated and took nothing without dishing it out in equal fashion. The big, strong Sigma Alphas were frustrated and surprised by the handling they were getting by the pass rush and by the blocking of the Phi Tau front line.

After the first half, the Phi Taus had the game in control. It was obvious that they were the better team. The noise from the Sigma Alpha sideline had diminished dramatically as the game started to wind down. The rest of the onlookers and the opposing Phi Taus were beyond cheering. They were screaming encouragement that, by now, was reinforced with pride and the unbelievable reality that the

Sigma Alpha supermen had met their match in a "geek house."

There was only a minute left, and Phi Tau was ahead by three touchdowns, a runaway score. Phi Tau had the ball, and it was only a matter of time before it was all over. Ben was about to throw a short one to Denny, but saw a brief opening to the left as Clay broke clear down the sidelines. The ball was a real beauty. It flew from Ben's hand as if shot from a cannon. It had a tight spiral, on a line with little trajectory, hitting the hands of Clay Stevens with a thud. It was the only sound heard before the huge roar of the crowd at another Phi Tau touchdown. Everyone on the sidelines, except the Sigma Alpha fans, were jumping and screaming in celebration at the realization that they were witnessing an extraordinary day. Ben was all smiles as he turned his back to the field of play and raised his arms in victory.

It took only seconds for everything to dramatically change. Ben was hit from behind by the shoulder of Todd Worthington. The hit was late and unexpected, so his body had no defense to protect him from the fall. Ben hit the ground hard on his right shoulder. He heard and felt a pop that was accompanied by the excruciating pain of a broken bone. Ben was shocked by the pain and just lay prone until he sensed people around him trying to help him up and asking if he was okay. The crowds engulfed Ben, and there was great confusion as to what happened.

Meanwhile, Todd had slipped away unnoticed as the chaos intensified. He felt his familiar sense of gladness at accomplishing revenge for his own humiliation and loss of his superficial reputation. He was satisfied now that he had hurt and extinguished the force that had caused this undeniable embarrassment to his position and fraternity.

However, Todd Worthington did a great deal more than he may have anticipated. He had changed the fate of Benny David forever.

Chapter 15

The difficult winter was almost over. The wind off the lake had lost its bitter chill, and the days had more light and warmth to them. Ben was getting nervous about spring training starting in a few weeks, not sure how his throwing arm was going to perform. He had been to three doctors after his injury, and none of them had the experience to tell him if surgery would help his situation. The last was at the Northwestern Medical Center and was a specialist in the upper extremity. He was professor of orthopedics and had seen many fracture dislocations of the shoulder and had operated successfully on most. However, he didn't have the experience of operating on an elite athlete who needed to perform at high throwing levels.

Ben and his father listened to the indecisive verdict that maybe he would be able to perform as a major-league catcher, but more likely he would be unable to make the hard throws needed. The surgery was expensive, above the means of the David family, and Cincinnati would not pay for such "experimental" surgery on a young, unproven ballplayer.

It was after the initial injury that most of the damage was done. The local clinic doctor had taped and braced Ben's right arm close to his chest, preventing any movement for six weeks. At the time, this was the accepted treatment. But, this was not the correct way this injury should have been handled. Time would show that the inactivity had resulted in significant atrophy of the shoulder musculature. It was critical to operate immediately and then begin an aggressive rehabilitation program to get the strength and coordination back.

Afterward, Ben had used some weights and tried physical therapy, but nobody was able to tell him exactly what to do to recover to his previous throwing level. There was no specific rehabilitation program for him to follow, but Ben knew the final test would be when he was allowed to throw a ball.

At first, the results were disappointing, but with weeks of gradual throwing in the gym with his dad, he felt small gains in improvement. By the time he had to report to Tampa at the end of March for spring training, he was able to throw with power, but not with great control. He had to think about his target rather than just throwing to it. The previous involuntary accuracy was not there. Perhaps the coaches down at spring training could help him.

Ben arrived in Tampa the second week in March for spring training with the Reds, just after the winter quarter of final exams at Northwestern.

He was surprised by the heat and humidity of coastal Florida. This was a major change from the cold and wind of Chicago. He was sweating profusely as the cab dropped him off at the Hillsborough Hotel. The Hillsborough was an old hotel that had lost its prestige over the attrition of time. It was large and run-down, but it accommodated the Redleg players easily. All the minor-league players stayed at the Hillsborough, while the major-league club stayed at the newer and better equipped Hilton, with more modern comforts.

Ben checked in and found he was sharing a room with Flaco and Reno, his old Geneva teammates.

The room was large and had three spring cots laid out along the wall. There was only one dresser and a bathroom with a shower. It was on the tenth floor, with two large windows overlooking the main street below and the roof of the building across the street.

Ben was the first to arrive and settled in quickly to the sparse room. Within minutes, the door opened, and Reno stood in the threshold, meekly sticking his head through the door.

"Jesus, is this the pits or what!" he yelled, broadly smiling at Benny with his tall frame and dark, penetrating eyes.

Ben jumped up off the bed and ran over to greet his old battery mate.

"You look thinner," said Reno as he moved into the room and shook his hand.

Ben could see that Reno had put on some muscle over the winter, which looked good on his big frame. He looked more powerful and mature than Ben remembered.

"School and studying keep you away from the table?" said Reno with some concern to his tone.

Ben smiled and shot back, "Looks like you didn't hold back from the good life, too much money on fine wine and fancy desserts?"

The two pulled from the handshake and gave each other a hug that was a more appropriate greeting for two close friends.

Flaco arrived a short time later, and the three old teammates brought each other up to date on their winters. Flaco had spent the winter playing ball in Cuba and was in great shape from the experience. He also had put on some muscle and was more mature looking, sporting a small goatee. He still was quite thinly built, but the muscle gave him a very cut and anatomical appearance.

Reno had spent time in Luray, Virginia, his hometown in the Shenandoah Mountains. He hunted and fished with his father, becoming a very accomplished sharpshooter with the Colt revolver that he carried in a black leather holster when on the trails. It took no time for Reno to take out the Colt, strap it to his side, and stand defiantly in front of Ben and order him to clap his hands. Ben obliged, and before he could complete the clap, the Colt's barrel was stationed in between his hands.

"Do that again," he said, not believing what he had just seen, and Reno did it again, and again, before Ben gave up and accepted the situation.

Ben confided in them about his injury and the problems he was having feeling comfortable with the throw. Reno, who saw the concern and lack of confidence on Ben's face, tried to reassure him that all would be okay once they got out on the field and started to play ball.

The next day came quickly. The ballplayers had to be out on the field before eight. Pitchers and catchers started running short sprints after a warm-up of calisthenics and stretches. They then broke out into groups, and pitchers began throwing at progressive distances to the catchers. After about twenty minutes, Reno and Ben were at sixty feet, easily throwing to each other. Ben felt fine, but the throwing workout was very easy.

The afternoon was spent with batting practice, and Ben hit several shots out of the park on a line to right. There was no problem with his hitting.

Johnny Vee came over to the batting cage and watched Ben closely. He noticed the quickness and smoothness of his swing, being very impressed with the power and velocity that he generated. "Looking good, kid!" he yelled through the screen.

Ben smiled and nodded his thanks as he finished his turn.

Johnny Vee was famous for pitching two perfect games in one season when he pitched for the Reds twenty years ago. He never had another great year after that, but had a few good years in the majors before retiring and returning to coaching for the Reds. He was assigned to be the manager for the Tampa Tarpons, the Class A team that was part of the Florida State League. Vee was a tough and cagey manager. He knew what it would take for a player to make it in the majors. He especially knew how pitchers and catchers needed to perform and had great knowledge in finding and pitching to a batter's weakness.

Vee's problem was he was getting older and arthritic, walking with a bent-over hobble, and he smoked and drank too much. His body was wearing out, and he found it difficult to be active. He would usually find his spot at the end of the dugout and sit there the whole game, barking out orders and not moving except to confront an umpire upon a disputed call. It was well known that the game would be delayed for more than the usual five or six minutes when Vee had to slowly get out of the dugout and walk over to the ump, bellowing and spitting out his disagreement with a call. The umpires hated Johnny Vee. It was common for him to be thrown out of a game. Once he made the effort to get off his spot in the dugout and approach the field, it was a done deal. He didn't plan on doing this more than once a game. Every effort was focused on the fact that the only option available was "You're outta here, Vee" from the angry umpire.

As Ben walked out of the cage, Vee approached him in his familiar slow limp. "You're going to be my catcher this season, and I expect big things from you, kid." There was no smile from the very tan and wrinkled face of Vee, only serious authority. Ben felt intimidated by the matter-of-fact statement and could only stand there with a dumb-looking smile on his face as Vee abruptly turned and walked off without further comment.

The next two weeks went well for Benny. He hit the ball well, and there were no major demands on his throwing other than relaxed infield practice and warming up pitchers. He felt like he was getting into good shape. He would run with the pitchers who had to run sprints in the outfield every day. Catchers didn't have to run, but it made Ben feel good and helped relax him.

He did have some concern about his arm because it didn't feel like it did before his injury. It seemed "detached," not under his control, but if he concentrated on his target, he could get by with an adequate throw. It was not automatic anymore.

The first few games went well enough, but the pitchers were not throwing with all of their talents, and the games were low-key and more instructional, with managers and coaches trying to get the players to understand their positions and game plan strategies. When the weeks of spring training were about over, the team assignments were handed out, and Benny, Flaco, and Reno were going to Tampa with manager Johnny Vee.

Chapter 16

The first game for the Tampa Tarpons took place on a very hot and humid day. Al Lopez Field, the Tarpons' home field and the largest ballpark in the league, had diathermy-type waves rising from the dry, sandy infield. The crowd was large and almost to full capacity this opening day, anticipating the new season and seeing what their new Tarpons were like. The large crowd produced an ever-present machinelike hum, adding to the intensity and excitement the players felt as the teams took batting practice and warmed up.

Ben felt very nervous before the big crowd. He did not know how he was going to perform after the long winter layoff. Johnny Vee had picked Reno to start on the mound and Ben to be behind the plate. Ben noticed that Reno had very good movement on his fastball that had not been present before. The velocity generated by the added muscle of Reno's torso was evident as the pre-game warm-up started. The slider and curveball were the same as last season, but with the new speed on the fastball, this was not going to be a problem. After the pre-game activities, the home team took the field to thunderous applause.

The Tarpons were playing Saint Petersburg, the Yankee franchise, who always were good and in the running for the title.

The first three innings went well. Reno allowed only one hit and had five strikeouts. Ben had no problem throwing, but there were no major demands on his arm so far. At the plate, Flaco and Ben both had doubles, leading the team to a 1–0 score. In the bottom of the fourth inning, Reno walked his first batter and was into his stretch. As the motion committed to the plate, the runner on first took off for second. The pitch was wide and off-speed, forcing Ben to hasten his throw to second. As he released the ball, Ben knew it was bad. There was no pain, but more of a tightness and awareness that seemed foreign to the throwing motion that he had been so familiar with his whole life. The ball sailed two feet over Flaco's head, into center field, allowing the runner to take third. Reno and Flaco were dumbfounded and speechless, not expecting this from the boy with the "golden arm."

Ben was confused and embarrassed, glad he was wearing his catcher's mask to hide his flushed expression. After that, things got much worse. Ben started to concentrate too much, "thinking the throw" rather than just letting his autonomic nervous system do the job uninhibited from his higher cerebral brain centers. The usual throw back to the pitcher became a mental chore and phobia for Benny. He couldn't stop thinking that the throw would be off the mark. His throw-backs were all over the place, causing Reno to be jumping, squatting, reaching right and left to retrieve the ball from Ben. The runner on third took advantage of this, jogging home after Ben threw the ball over Reno's head. This tied the game, 1–1. The inning was finally over, and Ben ran rather than jogged back to the refuge of the dugout, thus avoiding the increasing jeers from the crowd.

Reno and Flaco came over with quizzical looks and questioned him with great concern. "*Que pasa amigo?*"

said Flaco, and "What the hell?" said Reno, both simultaneously in whispered voices.

"I don't know," said Ben with a quivering voice, almost in tears.

Johnny Vee observed all from his usual position at the front of the dugout and had no expression on his stern face.

The next inning came all too quickly for Benny. The throws back to the pitcher were better as Ben used his concentration and lobbed the ball in a very cautious manner. In the seventh inning, the Yankees' leadoff hitter hit a double, followed by Reno giving up a walk. There were now two on and nobody out. With the score 1–1, it was a bunt situation, so Flaco let both Reno and Ben know he would be the one to take the throw. The bunt was laid down just in front of the plate, and Ben was on it immediately. He whirled to fire the throw to Flaco at second, but saw he was too late to get the runner for the force, so he turned to first and threw with his usual power. However, the ball went flying over the first baseman's head, into right field, allowing one run to score and the runner to advance to third. The batter went on to second, and nobody was out.

The crowd responded with a loud initial groan followed by boos and jeers that didn't let up for a full five minutes. Reno just looked away, and Ben silently moved behind the plate in a state of remorseful shock. As the next hitter came up, Reno bore down with his fastball and slider, getting ahead of the count. Ben was so incapacitated by it all he could barely throw the ball with any authority back to Reno.

It was pathetic to watch. Reno was able to strike out the next two, and the third popped up to the infield to end the inning.

During the seventh-inning stretch, there was a pause in the game to allow a raffle to take place. A new Chevrolet was driven onto the field as the PA announced, "And now, ladies and gentlemen, a brand-new 1960 Chevrolet will be raffled off to a lucky fan."

The crowd silenced in anticipation of the winning number, and during this lull, a loud voice from behind the home team dugout yelled out, "Hell with the car, raffle off the catcher!"

There was a pause followed by thunderous laughter that sickened Benny David to his core. He had never had to be the "the goat." He was always the hero. Visibly shaken and confused, he was genuinely fearful of having to go out on the field again.

Johnny Vee had seen this scenario before. It was when an injury disrupted the involuntary movement of great players, destroying the built-in confidence, which led to indecision and doubt. He stood up and walked slowly over to Ben and whispered in his ear that he was taking him out of the game. Benny was relieved, but still very shaken and devastated by it all.

After the game, Johnny Vee called Ben into his office at the back corner of the locker room. He was gulping down a beer from his stock in the cooler next to his chair. He looked up as Ben entered and drawled, "Sit down, kid," with a Camel cigarette dangling from his lower lip. "Seems like your arm went dead on you today. What happened?"

Ben sat down and told Johnny all about his shoulder injury at school and how it had been cared for. "It hasn't been right since. I have no good control over my throw. I have to think about what I am doing, and it just tightens me all up."

Johnny sat looking at Ben with a serious grimace, not saying anything for the next two minutes. "Pro baseball is a very tough game, and you have to be tough to play it, both mentally and physically. You may overcome this, but we will have to see," he said finally. "For now, you are benched, and Lopez will take over the catching. You will have to figure this out, kid, and we will see."

Ben stood up and left, saying only, "Yes, sir," as he passed the unemotional Vee.

The next several weeks passed with no major changes in Ben's throwing situation. Johnny Vee had his coaches try to work with the basic forms and grips, but to no avail. Ben just couldn't get the force, velocity, and accuracy to come together and return him to his old form. His hitting was no problem, so Vee tried to put him in the outfield to keep him in the lineup. He hoped that the long throwing motion of the outfielder was different enough from the catcher's throw that a new position would be the answer. But, the new position was just too different in its demands. Ben couldn't cut it. He did not have the experience or the speed pro ball demanded to judge fly balls or cope with hard-hit grounders.

Reno tried to get Ben to relax more and, along with Falco, to get his mind on other things like drinking beer, looking for girls, and socializing, but Ben was too upset with himself and baffled by it all to go along with their attempts at helping him.

Ben knew he had to figure this out on his own. He would need to better understand the nature of his injury and how it was treated, or should have been treated, to overcome his dilemma. His emotions of embarrassment and depression kept growing. He became more introverted and quiet. His teammates started to leave him alone more, and all knew it was just a matter of time before Ben would be released.

It was the end of June when Johnny Vee called him into the office for a talk. "We have gone as far as we can go, kid. The front office has issued your release, and I can't disagree with them. It is a shame that such great talent and potential has been wasted. I'm not a doctor, but something wasn't done right with your arm. Maybe you will find someone who can help you recover, but Cincinnati won't spend the dough to find out. You're a rookie and untried. As of now, you are out on waivers, so there is a chance some other club will pick you up. My advice, kid, is go back to school, get your education, and move on. Your flight will be booked tomorrow, so get packed. Your locker here will be reassigned to the new catcher." Johnny Vee slowly stood up and extended his hand. "Good luck, kid."

Ben was not surprised, but still felt awkward as he shook Vee's hand and thanked him for all his help. He left that office a different young man, whose direction in life now had to change.

PART 2

Chapter 1

The Rocky Mountain Sports Medicine Institute was located high in the upper valley of Aspen, Colorado, a beautiful ski resort town that was known worldwide as a recreational playground and cultural mountain retreat. The institute had two main buildings and a small lodge for athletes on ten beautiful acres in the high country. The lodge had specially controlled rooms that could alter barometric pressure, enabling ambient oxygen content to be adjusted for different altitude environments, and a fully equipped kitchen and recreation room so athletes and athletic teams could be comfortably housed during the training and testing protocols the institute offered.

The two main buildings contained a fully equipped exercise physiology lab, including bio-mechanical, video, and HD computer systems, and treadmills of all sizes, not only for runners, but also for bikers and cross-country skiers. Next to the labs, there was a large area for exercise, including a regulation basketball court, indoor baseball batting cages, and a dirt infield. There were also an Olympic-sized swimming pool with flume, weight rooms, indoor track, and aerobic rooms. The institute, for its size, was the finest sports medicine facility in the world. Its main mission was to deal with sports performance problems or questions that were not injury related. Injuries were dealt with by the orthopedic group located in town at the Aspen hospital.

The institute was the brainchild of Dr. Ben David, who founded and had run it for the past thirty years. Dr. David became a pioneer in the field of sports medicine after his arm injury ended his career in professional baseball. He became a key organizer and researcher, as well as one of the first clinicians to use modern medical education and to apply techniques to help athletes perform better and safer in their sport. His interest and past sports experience, along with his formal medical training, had put him on a natural path for the sports medicine field.

He was the only physician on staff, but he had the help of Kyle Burton, an exercise physiologist, and Louis Marlo, a bio-mechanical and computer expert. There was a nurse, receptionist, and lab technician, as well as housekeepers, cooks, and maintenance personnel. There were always other physicians, fellows, and students about the place who were part of educational programs at universities and institutes from all over the world. Dr. David was famous and always in demand.

The changes that occurred in his life after his injury were all positive and productive, but he always had the deep regret that he could not accomplish his early dreams of playing in the major leagues.

After graduating from Northwestern, Ben entered medical school. When he was released by Cincinnati, he concentrated on his studies, finding the sciences to his liking. He excelled at the premed science curriculum, making the dean's list and Phi Beta Kappa at graduation. He had no trouble getting into the University of Cincinnati Medical School. His excellent grades and history of playing in the Cincinnati Reds farm system made him a favorable candidate, especially since the dean was a Reds fan.

Ben went on into medicine, eventually finishing a residency in internal medicine and a subspecialty of sports medicine.

He had lost touch with Reno and Flaco after he graduated from medical school, but their careers moved ahead in baseball. Reno was a Cy Young winner five years in a row for Cincinnati, and Flaco was a consistent all-star, eventually elected to the Baseball Hall of Fame.

It was at the induction ceremonies ten years ago that Ben last saw Reno and Flaco. They both looked out of shape at the time, but Flaco still had his skinny frame, with a small potbelly, and Reno, although twenty pounds overweight, still had his good looks and strong shoulders. Flaco was retired in Florida, and Reno was still active in baseball, managing the Reds for over fifteen years, then retiring, but recently coming out of retirement and being named as the manager for the new National League team in Denver, the Colorado Rockies.

Ben was back in his office after the successful weekend running of the Leadville Trail 100. He had his blood drawn that morning by his lab tech, Nancy, to check his enzymes and chemistries so he could compare them to previous ultra runs, and to see if his glycolysis enzyme and polymer drink had done their jobs in ways he could measure objectively. He knew they were successful from his subjective impressions.

Ben had become very active in aerobic sports. When he was at school and baseball was out of the picture, he began running. At first it was 10Ks, then marathons, and eventually ultra-marathons. Running over fifty miles at a time became his forte. He was successful in finishing these grueling races in good shape and with good times. Running, then and now, was his best tension reliever and coping mechanism during the tight schedules that his medical training required. This running and training resulted in excellent fitness levels for him.

Through the years, he continued not only to be an active participant, but made it a subject of intense interest to study and research during his medical career. During the long winters in Aspen, cross-country skiing became the main fitness activity that stimulated his interest. He became quite good at it and enjoyed the smooth gliding, almost dancing, action through the beautiful Colorado snow. He had published several research papers on cross-country skiing performance and become an expert consultant in this area for coaches and team physicians worldwide.

His current schedule was jammed full with the men's US biathlon team. They were here for the week to undergo physiological testing before the winter competitive season. It was a sport consisting of cross-country skiing and rifle marksmanship. As a group, they were the fittest of all aerobic athletes because of the metabolic demands of maximizing aerobic performance from both the arms and the legs. Biathlon, which not only demands the most from aerobic endurance performance, also demands an opposite discipline. It demands the accuracy of the neuromuscular system to immediately turn down the high cardiovascular activities of skiing around a tough up-and-down course and hold a heavy rifle and shoot accurately at targets in standing and prone positions. The need to slow the heart rate after it has been fast for several minutes, and then control muscle precision so the eye and neuromuscular coordination allow the athlete to hit a target in a calm manner, requires the utmost in physical performance discipline. These were truly unique athletes.

The first biathlete was getting his cardiac monitoring electrodes put on, and Kyle Burton, the exercise physiologist, was warming up the metabolic cart and getting out the face mask so aerobic capacity could be measured throughout the test. The athlete would have on a mask to measure oxygen uptake and carbon dioxide production, a finger stick device on the finger to measure lactates, a cardiac monitor to watch and record heart rate, and a sphygmomanometer to measure blood pressure. The athletes would skate ski on the large Nordic treadmill with their roller skis and rubber-tipped poles, simulating the actual skiing technique required in competition.

Duncan Malone was the biathlete getting ready for the test as Ben walked in. "Hi, Dunc, feeling strong today?" he said with a smile on his face.

Duncan didn't offer a friendly reply other than a brief "yeah" in anticipation of the pain that was about to come. He was the best on the team. He could push himself harder than any of the other gifted athletes, getting into and staying in the pain zone the longest. He seemed to relish the agony as the demands got harder. He took his training seriously and committed himself to the yearlong training required to be world class in this sport.

Kyle had the treadmill going at the initial warm-up speed as Duncan began the smooth arm and leg motion of the skating technique. After a few minutes of warm-up, Duncan's pace began to pick up as the speed and grade of the treadmill increased. Blood pressure and pulse, as well as oxygen consumption, began going up, until Duncan was working very hard. Ben noticed that the oxygen uptake was at a plateau now, and the lactate levels started to spike. It would only be a few seconds more before Duncan would get anaerobic and have to stop.

"Ready to stop, Dunc?" asked Ben, expecting a confirmatory nod of the head.

Surprisingly, there was no nod. Duncan kept pushing hard and not showing signs of giving up. He was now way past the expected stop point, not giving the shake of the head to indicate he wanted to stop. The treadmill kept getting faster and going higher as Duncan kept up the pace. Ben was very surprised at how far past the max Duncan was pushing himself. He knew the pain, as indicated by the lactate buildup, was very high. He had not seen any athlete reach this pain point and keep going. Duncan should have stopped a few minutes ago.

"Keep going, Dunc?" asked Ben, this time with some anxiety in his voice, looking at Kyle, who also had a very surprised expression on his face.

No confirmation from Duncan, who was struggling now, but not giving the head nod to stop. Suddenly there was a crash. It happened in seconds, before Kyle or Ben could react. Duncan went flying off the back of the treadmill as electrode wires and the face mask tube broke away. He crashed into the expensive metabolic cart, dispersing equipment all over the room. Kyle quickly turned off the treadmill, and Ben rushed over to Duncan to see if he was okay.

"Jeez, are you all right?" said Ben, picking up Duncan from the mess.

Duncan gave a smile and said, "Yep, no problem," from his position on the floor.

This was the first time anyone had fallen off a treadmill during one of his tests, and Ben was a bit shaken up by it all. "I never expected this, Duncan. You gave no indication you were going to stop."

Duncan got up slowly as Ben got the roller skis off. "I was not near my max pain point," he said, "and I wanted to know where my max was."

Ben realized he had a fantastic competitor here who had the mental makeup to win. He did not have the highest oxygen uptake on the team, but had more than enough to make up for that. "You did great, Duncan. We will have the complete results for you tomorrow," said Ben with a laugh.

Duncan went to the showers, not hurt, but amused by all the concern the doc and Kyle showed.

Kyle walked over to Ben with the printouts in his hand. "This kid would be a great candidate for the enzyme cartridge. With his willpower and the boost the enzyme would have for his VO2 max, it would put him on the podium."

Ben was thinking the same thing, when Annie, his receptionist, ran in. "There is a Mr. Reno DeAngelo on the phone who needs to talk to you right away. He said he was an old friend and this was very important."

What could this be about? thought Ben as he left Kyle to grab the phone in his office.

Ben's office was like a museum. The walls were covered with autographed photos of professional and Olympic athletes. The bookshelves were crowded not only with books, but various pieces of well-used athletic equipment that filled up any available space. File cabinets were stuffed with papers that prevented the doors from closing flush, and Ben's desk was cluttered with several odd-looking computer and machine parts that seemed to be waiting for more attention.

Rosie, a big black Newfoundland, lay sprawled out in the corner on an old baseball chest protector that had some of its stuffing sticking out of the side. She picked up her head slightly to acknowledge Ben's entrance into the room.

"Hello, Reno!" said Ben after he hurried into the room and picked up the phone.

"Hey Benny, glad you were in. I know you didn't expect a call from me, buddy, but you are the only guy on the planet that can help me." Reno got right to the point of his call. Ben didn't have to say much in the first several minutes, as Reno did all the talking.

"You probably know, Benny, that I am now the new CEO and acting manager of the Colorado Rockies. As a team, the Rockies have been piss poor, never getting out of the cellar in their division since coming into the league four years ago. I have been given this position by the owners to get results pronto! They are paying me a shit load and giving me the liberty of making all the decisions concerning the team. It is a dictatorship, and I am the dictator! I am pulling out all the stops. But, I need your help. You have a great reputation in the sports medicine area, and you are an old friend that I can trust. I feel there are ways that science and medicine can help us be a better team, even though I don't have a clue as to how. Baseball is way behind in this regard, and I was hoping you could fill in some of the blanks." Before Ben could answer, Reno went on. "I want to meet face-to-face, and I can be out on tomorrow's early plane to meet. What do ya say? Can you help an old buddy?"

Ben had the US biathlon team to deal with all week, but quickly figured a few hours of meeting with Reno was the least he could do, and frankly, he was excited about the potential of the project.

"You bet, Reno. Come on out. You can stay at the Jerome in Aspen, and we can meet tomorrow afternoon."

"Great, Benny, if I get any snags, I'll let you know. See ya tomorrow."

Ben hung up and quickly fell back in his char with an audible sigh. Slumped in his chair, he looked over at Rosie and put his feel up on the well-worn desk. "Well, Rosie, this could be big," he said prophetically as a very big smile came across his face.

Ben had always carried a burr under his saddle that he'd never made it in baseball. It was a disappointment to his father, and to Ben himself. The early predictions of greatness that his teammates and managers had for him fell short. In his own mind, Ben felt there was a failure of expectation, even though he had great successes in medicine and sports science. Throughout his career, he had always experimented with ideas he had concerning baseball and his own injury. In fact, it was the motivating factor that guided Ben into the field of sports medicine. How different things could have been for him if today's science was available.

Now, after all these years, he was going to get the opportunity to apply some of these ingenious plans he had. He did not know specifically what Reno was expecting of him, but Reno had no idea of the plans Ben had for the two of them and the Colorado Rockies. Reno was in for a big surprise.

Chapter 2

The short flight from Denver to Aspen was a bit rough. The mountains were having stormy and windy weather, which caused Reno to feel nauseated and sweaty. When the plane finally landed, he was the first to stand up and get out of the small aircraft, rushing ahead of an elderly woman who gave him a very angry look.

Reno entered the Aspen Airport wiping the sweat off his forehead and almost missed seeing Annie, Ben's secretary, holding a sign with his name on it.

"Hi, I'm Reno DeAngelo," he said in a loud voice.

Annie was surprised he was the first one off, but quickly smiled and guided him through the airport to her car. "Any luggage?" she said with a smile.

"No, it's a quick trip. I've got all I need in here," he said, pointing to his carry-on duffel. Annie noticed that the duffel was well used and guessed it was the one he'd used for years as a ballplayer.

It was late, so Annie took Reno to the Hotel Jerome, a remodeled Victorian beauty that was located in the center of Aspen. "You are all checked in. They have an excellent restaurant, so enjoy. I will be by to pick you up at eight and take you out to the institute."

Reno waved good-bye and entered the old, luxurious lobby of the Jerome.

The next morning, after a restless night's sleep, Reno woke up with a headache. He felt a little better after a shower and a light breakfast, but he still felt out of sorts as Annie picked him up at eight o'clock sharp.

Annie was pleasant on the drive out, but Reno couldn't respond in a similar fashion because of his headache. He also felt a bit short of breath, noticing it even more as he had to walk up several stone steps to the entrance of the institute.

Annie led him through a long glass corridor that looked into well-equipped workout rooms that lined both sides. Very fit young men and women were using the equipment with vigorous effort as enthusiastic coaches barked encouragement.

"They are the US biathlon team. They're here for the week undergoing testing and altitude training before their season begins on the Dachstien," said Annie, trying to answer a question before it was asked.

Reno looked confused. "What is the Dachstien?"

"Oh, it's a glacier in Austria that the team uses to start early snow training and skiing on," Annie said with a smile. Reno followed her as if in a dream state, puzzled by it all.

Reno was led into Ben's office and gasped as Rosie the Newfoundland rushed over and put her head right into his crotch. A familiar voice laughed as Reno backed up quickly and said, "What the hell!"

"It's her way of greeting old friends, Reno. She won't bite," said Ben cheerfully. The two old battery mates looked at each other with big smiles and hugged as each said, "Good to see you, buddy," simultaneously.

Ben saw that Reno still looked a bit out of shape, carrying about fifteen pounds of extra weight. He still had those broad, strong-looking shoulders, tall posture, and handsome features that Ben remembered. His hair was full, but graying at the sides, and his face had gained some wrinkles.

Reno could see that Ben had kept his athletic build and even looked lean and more muscular than he did when he played baseball. "You're keeping yourself in good shape, Benny. You look fantastic for an old fart," he said with a smile.

"I work at it, Reno. Working out keeps me happy and sane. Plus, I like to try out my research products on myself before I let others use them."

Reno sat down and looked straight at Ben. "That's why I am here, Ben. I am hoping that you may be able to help us. We need to be at a higher level of play than we have been at. Our players are young and talented, but something is lacking. Maybe it's inexperience, maybe we are not doing the right things, but we need to win. I am under the gun to make it happen, with my reputation on the line. Can you see yourself helping us win? Educate me!" said Reno loudly.

Ben did not respond quickly. He sat back in his chair and smiled for several seconds.

"What is that shit-eating grin for? You look like a man that has a secret he is thinking about spilling," said Reno. "What's up? Tell me fast. This headache has been with me all morning, and I have little patience."

Ben sat up straighter in his chair and acknowledged his friend's impatience. He quickly stood up and ran from the room. "I'll be right back," he said as the door closed behind him.

He returned in a few seconds with an oxygen cylinder and nasal cannula. "You have an altitude headache. Because you came up to eight thousand feet from near sea level so quickly, the hypoxia that occurs here is causing your arterioles to dilate. They dilate to enable more oxygenated blood to get to your tissues. The dilated arterioles will push on nerve bundles in the perivascular space, and this will cause pain." As he was talking, he put the nasal cannula into Reno's nose and started the flow at three liters per minute.

Reno didn't understand a word Ben was saying, but he immediately felt the headache dissipate as the oxygen flowed in. He was amazed at all this and could only look at Ben with a dumb look on his face, nodding up and down at his esoteric words.

Ben could see the effects of the oxygen immediately. The color of Reno's complexion improved and his eyes had a sharper look to them as the hypoxia cleared.

"I feel much better, Benny," said Reno weakly.

Ben just smiled as he sat back in his chair and started to answer Reno's questions in a slow and serious manner. "Frankly, Reno, I've been waiting for this opportunity for a long time. It started when my baseball career ended and I went into medicine. Over the years, with help from Kyle and Louie, my associates here, I've come up with many ideas. The motivation is, and has been, to help other athletes who have been sidelined in sports because of circumstances beyond their control. We want to understand how to help players improve their performance safely.

"My fantasy of playing ball again in the majors has prompted many of these projects. Some are quite effective, while others still need some time to perfect. Your visit today may be the chance to apply them in the real world."

Reno looked at Benny. "I am not interested in having my team be a bunch of guinea pigs, Benny. This is the big leagues, no time for screw-ups here."

Benny just smiled. "Reno, you and I go way back. What I am about to say will sound crazy, but hear me out." He began a long explanation of his plans for the three old-timers to play baseball again and help the Rockies win games. The science available now, and some of the techniques that Ben had discovered, could make this fantasy happen.

Reno sat quietly as he heard what Ben had to say before he spoke. "You have traveled to another planet, my friend.

I have not heard anything so preposterous and off-the-wall. This is crazy!"

Benny noticed Reno's hesitant look as he went on about the nuttiness of the plan.

"Wouldn't it be wonderful to be able to go back and try again? We were the best prospects in those days. You and Flaco had your time in the big show, and both of you were successful. I didn't get to be with you then, but now it can happen with the science we have."

"Well, Flaco was a helluva lot more successful than me. He is in the Hall. Besides, we are old men, and this can't happen now." Reno got up, finishing the meeting. He looked at Ben and just shook his head. He took off the oxygen cannula and went to the door. "Let's have dinner tonight after I think about this some more. I need a nap. This is nuts!"

Ben led Reno out to the front desk and arranged for him to get back to the hotel. "I'll meet you at the Jerome at six thirty. Rest up, and I will go into more detail then."

Reno waved as Annie drove him out of the institute on a steep driveway that descended to the road that led to town.

Ben had outlined the science and research he had done that would apply to Reno's request. He had outlined the state-of-the-art information that could legally help the Rockie ballplayers to improve their performance. However, he had stepped into another realm when he began to explain the idea that he, Reno, Flaco could contribute to the success of the Rockies by their own performances. Ben knew the projects he had developed may not be fully understood, or felt to be kosher by the league officials. The projects were now at the point of being tried, but because they were untested under real circumstances, there was a certain risk to the players who used them. It was because of the uncertain nature of these projects that Ben felt he would have to take on the full responsibility himself. Therefore, he had to be included in the project, and hoped Reno, and maybe Flaco, would involve themselves in this very uncertain and potentially risky business. Certainly, Ben knew this whole situation was motivated by his own self-interest from missing out on his major league hopes. However, the advancement of sports medicine as a discipline needed to be applied to performance-enhancing techniques that would be safe, effective, and legal. The legality would be the unknown factor until the science became accepted as the "usual and customary" practice of baseball. Ben knew he had a hard sell for Reno, and possibly Flaco, as he finished up at the institute and headed into town for dinner.

The lobby of the Jerome was majestic in its Victorian furnishings and old wood panels. Reno was waiting for Ben in front of the marble-lined fireplace, looking more comfortable than he had earlier.

Reno had had a long afternoon nap, and his headache was gone. He had several questions about Ben's plan, but felt excited about the possibility of a second chance for him at the age of sixty-five.

"I may be crazy, Benny, but I'm going to go with you on this, at least until I am convinced one way or the other that this is going to work. You know this is going to be laughed at by all of baseball when they hear about us thinking of a comeback."

Ben nodded his head in agreement. "Why don't we start out with you and I in the program for the next few months? You'll see how this works and have a good idea if we should go ahead. Just give me at least six weeks, no strings attached."

This sounded reasonable to Reno. The two shook hands and entered the dining room of the Jerome.

Chapter 3

Only a week passed, and Reno found himself back in Aspen to start Ben's program. The initial strategy was for Reno to get back in shape and lose weight. Ben had outlined a low-fat and low-carbohydrate diet, no alcohol, and a series of training exercises to improve his strength, endurance, and coordination. The sessions started out very slow. Ben knew it would take six weeks of base training before Reno felt comfortable with more advanced training. The plan was to begin the training indoors under direct supervision by Ben or Kyle so proper form was used and the intensity of Reno's effort could be monitored correctly. This would be necessary to gain the most out of the training and minimize the chance of overtraining and injury. Ben was starting with a sedentary sixty-five-year-old man, but Reno had the athletic potential to progress rapidly.

Reno went through a comprehensive physical exam, full exercise stress testing, and neuromuscular-bio-mechanical evaluations. His general health was excellent, his strength and coordination testing was good, but his aerobic condition was poor. Working with this data, Kyle formulated an exercise prescription that would be the most effective for Reno's baseline condition. Isokinetic and weight- resistant exercises were done daily, using different muscle groups in alternating fashion.

Yoga, stretching, and balance exercises were done daily as well. Intensity, duration, and frequency of the aerobic exercise was strictly monitored and controlled at each session. The treadmill, elliptical, and stationary bike, Versa Climber, Nordic tTrack, and rowing machine were all utilized as various endurance disciplines. The meals were also controlled in content but were very well prepared and presented.

At first Reno had a hard time adapting to the demands of the daily training. Ben and the staff were patient with him, but took no excuses for varying from the routine. Eventually, after the first two weeks, Reno began to enjoy the feeling of being physically active again. The exercise was gauged to fit his baseline fitness exactly, causing him to never feel overstrained or fatigued, even though he was worked hard. Reno found the whole program of exercise and nutrition, and the atmosphere of the institute, to be invigorating. His basic physical being was awakening, which he found to be a very gratifying and pleasing experience.

In the first few weeks, Reno was a bit stiff, but nothing that was troublesome or uncomfortable. His weight began to fall off faster than he'd anticipated. He could see his strength and endurance improve daily. However, he still didn't see how this was going to get him into major-league playing shape.

After the first six weeks of very hard work, Ben could see Reno was ready for the advanced program. At breakfast, Reno joined Ben, Kyle, and Louie in the cafeteria. Ben started out the discussion with a funny grin on his face.

"You're ready now for the real work, Reno. You have developed a strong base without injury, and you have improved all of your performance parameters extremely well. Now it's time to move on to the phase that's going to count and be much tougher on you. It will be geared more specifically to the goal of playing big-time baseball again."

"I was waiting for this day to come. I do feel like a million bucks thanks to your training program, Benny, and thank you, thank you all for getting me here. I appreciate how good it feels to be in shape again, but frankly, I don't see how you can make this fantasy project happen. I will get our players into your training program so they can get very fit before spring training, but c'mon, guys, I am nowhere near the caliber of my players."

Ben became very serious and looked over at Kyle and Louie before answering. "You're right, Reno, and it is certain that having the team here before spring training would be a great help in starting the season right. But, the advances in sports medicine, especially the progress we have made here at our Aspen institute, have much more to offer than the standard approaches of getting in great shape."

Ben then began to go into a brief description of what he had in mind for the next several weeks. "I am going to ask you to do some things that you will be skeptical about at first, but you must trust me that it will make sense later on. Also, you will be pushed harder than you would expect from your old buddy Benny, and may question the tactics you're going through. However, for all of us to be successful, I need you to make the commitment and try to do what we ask even if it seems strange to you."

Reno looked at the group and could see that they were very serious and anxious about what was coming next. "Benny, you are making me nervous now," he said with a laugh.

However, this did not change the tension at the table as they all looked at Reno without smiling.

"Look, this was all a crazy idea to my way of thinking, but I have shown up, done the work, and followed your plans, so let's move on. I am curious to see what you have in mind, fellas." Reno was truly nervous, but he trusted Ben implicitly.

After they all finished eating breakfast, Ben led the group into a large room that Reno had never seen before. It was equipped with a batting cage, pitching mound, and several unusual-looking pieces of equipment that were unfamiliar.

"Let me give you a little tour," said Ben with the pride of a young boy showing off his new car.

The batting cage faced a large movie screen that was situated behind the pitching mound. It could project a video of any top pitcher in the league, simulating the motion of the pitcher with the mechanics of the pitching machine. It appeared as if the pitcher on screen actually was throwing the pitch. In addition, the machine could throw fastballs at various speeds, as well as curveballs, sliders, change-ups, and split-finger fastballs, all from the right or left hand. Louie Marlo, the bio-mechanical and computer genius, had programmed the machine to deliver the specific movement that the individual pitcher could put on the ball and control it to anywhere in the strike zone. It was a marvel.

"Go ahead, Reno. Give it a try. Step in," said Ben as he handed Reno a bat.

It was amazing how realistic it was for Reno to be facing the great Umberto Gonzales, the starting ace for the rival Chicago Cubs.

"How about a fastball on the inside corner?" said Ben as Reno took his stance.

The video played, showing Umberto going into his windup, and *zoom*, the ball flew out of his hand to the inside corner of the plate. Reno was amazed at the realism of the Simulator. "Damn, that's incredible!" he said with the bat on his shoulder.

Ben didn't waste any time and quickly started over to another area. "C'mon, over here. Let me show you my pride and joy, Reno," he said as he led him over to a platform that had several bodysuits hanging on rods that looked like rubberized, pressurized suits similar to what jet pilots wear. They had several tubes and wires that hung from the arms and torso, and other wires that were attached to the legs. "I had this one made to your measurements, Reno. Try it on."

Reno was helped by Kyle as he got into the suit. It was snug and fitted him like a Lycra bodysuit that Nordic skiers wear. Louie attached the wires to a large bank of computers, and Ben led Reno over to the pitcher's mound.

"Take this ball, and here's a mitt. Go ahead and give your windup to the plate." Ben got behind the plate with his catcher's mitt to receive the ball.

Reno went through his motion gingerly, not knowing what to expect.

"No, give it a full windup, and throw as if you mean it!" yelled Ben behind the plate.

Reno could feel a strange loss of his muscle control as the suit seemed to take over the movement of his motion. He felt an out-of-body experience as he went into the throw to the plate. The ball fired from his hand, toward the center of Ben's mitt, hitting it with a loud crack. Reno almost fell over, not believing what had just happened.

Ben started laughing at Reno's shocked surprise. "Your throw was controlled by the stimulating electrodes in the suit that fired and contracted the appropriate musculature. This was programmed in the computer by Louie. The computer inputs your baseline neuromuscular patterns of firing, analyzes your muscle latent periods and contraction strength, then overrides your individual delays from higher centers that prevent the smooth, efficient action of the throw. It's individualized specifically to your physiology. Over these next several weeks, we must train your throwing musculature to get stronger, smoother, and awaken those latent fibers that have been inactive for so many years. You will relearn to throw your fastball, curve, slider, and change-up using this suit. Much will be up to you as you go through the training, but you can see the advantage that this computerized suit will have in getting you on the mound for the Rockies."

Reno was totally dumbfounded. He obviously could see the potential that Ben could open up. The power excited him, but he needed to know more.

Ben explained how he developed the computerized suit to solve the problem he had after losing the power and accuracy of his own throw. It took a long time waiting for some of the technology to be available, but it also took the genius of Louie Marlo, his bio-mechanist and computer guy, to give his input for the final touches.

Ben also showed Reno a batting simulator that could coordinate the swing more efficiently, especially when it was used with the video pitching machine. It also consisted of the rubberized suit that was connected to Louie's computer bank.

Finally, Ben showed him a rotating batting swing machine called the Rotator. This device produced isokinetic resistance to the batting swing, allowing improved torsional strength and power. This could also be dovetailed with the computerized batting suit.

It all seemed so surreal to Reno. Was all this legal? There was nothing like this in baseball.

"This is the future, Reno," said Ben, almost reading his mind. "I have wanted to use this science for quite a while now. Sure, we can expect problems because I don't know how you will react to the training needed for these machines to work well. It is an experiment. That's why I had planned that you, Flaco, and I would be the lab rats in all this. I would have to keep your team out of all this except for some of the basic training and nutrition aspects, the Simulator and the Rotator. The suits would only be for our use. We have to establish a very workable model that has all the kinks worked out. Until we can be sure the league will accept these concepts, this knowledge has to be kept private. We have an obligation to be sure it is effective, safe, and most importantly, that the methods will be accepted as legal."

Reno agreed as Ben was talking, and would go along with the project as Ben outlined it. He could see, however, that the notion of three old men playing major-league base-ball, and playing well enough to help the Rockies win the World Series, would be a joke—a joke that he would have a very hard time selling to the owners and to the league. Hell, he was the "dictator" and had full authority for the club this year, but still, it was nuts.

"Okay, Ben, I see this is going to be really big. I have to organize a few things from my end. We have some red tape and some financing to consider for all this to happen. If it can happen." His mind raced as he thought about some of the hurdles he would have to jump. He had to get back to Denver, but reassured Ben he would be back in a few days to start the program. "I'll also see if I can get hold of Flaco. He is down in Miami, and it will take a trip down there to fill him in and see if he is okay with all this."

Ben shook his head. "No, it is too early to contact Flaco. I want you and me to spend the next four to six weeks work-ing on this before we bring Flaco on board. Besides, when he sees the results of our work, it will be much easier to con-vince him to join us."

Ben drove Reno to the airport himself. They both were excited and nervous about what lay ahead. There were several unknowns, and it still seemed so crazy, but the pros-pect of playing again, and playing together on the same team again, forced them to overlook the risks and potential embarrassment that could ruin both their professional repu-tations and careers. There was little thought of turning back now.

Chapter 4

Ben was sitting in his office looking over the schedules that Kyle and he had worked out for Reno and himself. It was a concern that Reno would need maximum efforts to improve his muscle mass and strength. He would need a major step-up of his endurance training, and coordination exercises. Kyle was dubious that he would be able to accomplish this in such a short period of time.

"He does have a strong frame and is fairly coordinated, but he may not have enough time to get to where the Simulator and Rotator will have the desired effect. You have been working on your fitness for years now, Ben, and he is nowhere near the levels that you are."

Ben agreed, but felt he had no choice but to move ahead. Time was running out. "If we have to use the enzyme converter to get his levels up, we will. I have confidence in it after using it at the Leadville 100. It made a big difference, and I think it will allow him to step up the volume and intensity of his training without causing him to overtrain or get injured."

Kyle gave a thumbs-up as he stood up and stumbled over Rosie, who was lying at the foot of Ben's desk. She didn't even look up as Kyle dropped all his papers to the floor as he grabbed the edge of the desk to keep his balance. It certainly broke the tension in the room as both men laughed at the big black Newfie.

The early fall morning in the Colorado Rockies was very cool and brisk. The colors of the changing aspens against the majestic snow-sprinkled mountaintops and blue Colorado sky were a photographer's dream. Ben and Reno had needed to dress in the full outfit of polypro tights and jacket, stocking hat, and gloves to stay warm as they started out on a fourteen-mile trail run from the institute to town on the Government Trail.

The trail was popular for runners and mountain bikers, but at this early hour, it was deserted. Starting out, Ben kept the pace slow, knowing it would be difficult for Reno to get his footing on the rocky trail. Ben had been over this trail many times with his own training through the years and knew it could be treacherous. The time for indoor exercise was over. The pair had to start a major program of trail running and biking to put some risk into the aerobic work. This type of training would teach the body to understand when to be cautious and when to vary muscle activity to accommodate changing conditions, thus causing a more comprehensive adaption to the demands of the exercise at hand. The changing demands of the task would pay off not only in endurance, but improve reaction time, diversify recruitment of different muscle groups, and involuntarily cause micro-changes at the proprioception level. This would not occur by just doing continuous, non-changing activity on the indoor exercise machines. There was also an element of adventure in running a mountain trail that made it enjoyable enough for the time to go by quickly. The runner would not notice the pain as much when the mind was occupied and involved with running a beautiful trail like this and keeping attention on not making a mistake that could result in a serious fall.

Midway in the run, Ben offered Reno a drink of pinkish liquid that he carried in a belt pack. "Take a swig of this. It will help."

The two stopped running and started to walk as Reno took gulps of the berry-flavored liquid. "What is this stuff? It tastes good, which I would not have expected when working so hard."

The two walked for a few minutes as Ben explained the physiology of his glucose polymer endurance drink. "When the body is exercising at seventy to eighty percent of aerobic max, blood flow is directed away from the intestinal tract to the peripheral muscular bed. The muscle needs the oxygen and a glucose source to maintain muscular work. If they are not supplied in enough quantity, then fatigue and actual muscle pain will occur. Therefore, an en route feed that will supply the necessary fluid and carbohydrate to the muscle during prolonged exercise, or exercise that lasts more than sixty minutes, is a necessary habit to get into for maintaining a competitive pace. Water alone won't do it," said Ben emphatically.

Ben explained that the polymer drink would supply the maximum carbohydrate that could be absorbed from the gastrointestinal tract while hard exercise was occurring. The fluid-and-carbohydrate mixture would prevent the depletion and dehydration that could occur with long efforts. The taste was important as well. If it didn't taste good, the athlete would not drink it in the amounts needed to prevent depletion. The taste buds changed as the air of breathing rapidly passed over the tongue, making most harsh concentrated drinks taste too sweet or overbearing. Therefore, the formula that had been developed consisted of a berry flavor that had the right chemical proportions so the taste continued to be pleasing as hard exertion continued. The polymer drink was a big hit with endurance runners, skiers, and bikers. Ben had made it available to a select group of athletes he had tested.

As the two jogged along into town, the trail steepened, making the exocentric demands on the quads a new experience for Reno.

"Don't pound it too hard on the downhill even if you feel the relief of going down."

Reno could sense that the running was easier now that the uphill sections were over. He slowed his pace even though he felt good and could have run faster. In a few miles, he could feel his quads starting to quiver and weaken. Ben was right; downhill running had its demands that uphill running did not have. It could sneak up on you if you went out too hard.

Reno finished the run in good shape, although he was tired.

"We'll know we are in great shape when we can just turn around and head back the way we came," said Ben.

There was no way Reno could see himself ever doing that. He had no doubt, however, that Ben could have turned around and probably run the trail back faster than he had come.

Ben finally said, "Let's go eat some carbs so we replenish our glycogen stores as quickly as possible. The muscle enzymes are just begging for a load of carbohydrates after a run like this, and will load in more glycogen than if we wait to eat. We should be carbo-loading within the next thirty minutes."

They headed over to the Jerome for the pancake and waffle breakfast. "Now this is a training method I can get used to, Benny," said Reno happily as they jogged into the Jerome for the hearty breakfast of carbs.

Ben was pleased with Reno's progress over the next few weeks. He was able to tolerate the aerobic workouts without needing too much recovery, and he had no overuse injuries. It was especially pleasing to see him put on the simulator suit, get on the mound, and fire substantial fastballs and sliders.

Ben and Reno worked together in all aspects of the training. They improved their batting strength and power with the Rotator. They improved their throwing power and accuracy with the computerized suits. They kept up basic endurance and resistance training daily. It all prepared them for the actual demands needed to play baseball at a very high level. They were turning into athletes, which was an obvious change for Reno in the small amount of time that had passed since the start of the program.

The pitch-catch warm-up sessions were fun for both. It was a treat to experience the activity that they had done so often so many years ago. They were at a point now where their performance was on par with the time they had spent with the Geneva Redlegs. Ben had used the computerized throwing and batting suits for some time before Reno was on board, but Reno was a fast learner, progressing rapidly, making his pitches more accurate and having good movement on the ball every day. His endurance, however, did limit his ability to continue throwing for more than ten or fifteen batters. He was limited to about fifty pitches before he pooped out. Ben thought this would take some time, but again, he knew there was only so much to expect from a man his age.

It was very interesting for Kyle and Louie to watch the progress of these two old men utilizing these innovative techniques. They were like kids engaged in gym class, enthusiastic with their activities and progress. The return of familiar feelings that they had when they were younger athletes was an invigorating experience that Reno and Ben relished.

Ben had perfected his swing velocity, which now matched those of other current major-league hitters, and his throw from home to second was now almost perfect. Reno had a natural pitching windup and delivery that was magnified by the effects of the computerized suits. In time, it was hoped that after the suits recruited the proper muscle firing, Reno would develop the strength and efficiency needed to throw a tough pitch to hit. After six weeks of very good progress, Ben knew it was time to get Flaco.

Chapter 5

La Firma was Flaco Hernandez's upscale nightclub, located in the trendy South Beach area of Miami. It was always a crowded place, but this was especially true on Saturday night. That was the night Ben and Reno arranged to meet Flaco to explain their extraordinary plan for the first time.

La Firma was decorated in the latest and most modern of styles, typical for this area of South Beach. It had a large chrome bar with red-and-white plastic counters and mirrored shelves that held colored bottles of various sizes and shapes. The ceiling had neon tube lights that pulsated in time with the loud salsa music. The dance floor was crowded with men wearing tight black slacks and ballooning white shirts, almost as if in a uniform of some sort. The women wore low-cut blouses and high-cut skirts that many of them wore too tightly for their weight. The place was noisy, but it was where Flaco wanted to meet when Reno had called to set up the meeting.

Flaco had tried to get Reno to say why they were meeting, but Reno wanted to wait until they were face-to-face. Flaco hadn't seen Reno in years, but had talked with him on the phone when he took over the Rockies. He had toyed with the idea of being a bench coach for Reno and give up the Miami night scene, having grown tired with it. Reno was noncommittal at the time, but said he would keep the option open. Flaco assumed that maybe this was what the meet would be about. However, why all the secrecy, and why Benny David? He knew Ben was a doctor somewhere in the mountains, but had really lost touch with him. Flaco grabbed his single malt and went back to his office to get away from the crowd and noise.

Ben and Reno arrived at La Firma after a quick check-in and freshen-up at the Miami Beach Hilton. They were greeted at the door and escorted through the loud bar and dance floor by a thick-necked, muscular Asian man who said very little. He knocked loudly on the thick mahogany door of Flaco's office.

The door was opened by a tall, smiling, gray-haired, well-dressed Hispanic man smoking a large Cuban cigar. Ben met the eyes of his old teammate and recognized him immediately.

"Bennny," said Flaco, giving Ben a big hug.

"It's been too long, amigo," said Ben with emotion.

"Let me look at you two! You guys look fantastic, so fit looking and young. What's the secret? *Diga me todos amigos.*"

Flaco offered his two old friends a seat and opened his thirty-year-old scotch and poured each a drink. "*Salute*, to old times, *mi amigos.*" As the three took the toast, they relived some old times and spent several minutes catching up on their current situations before Reno got into why they were here.

Reno left very little out as he described how he came to call Ben for help to get his Rockies in better shape for the season and see if there was more they could learn from the modern medical and science information that was available to improve their performance. He described the institute in Aspen and how Ben had introduced him to the newer sports medicine techniques firsthand.

After Reno finished giving the background, he turned to Ben with a grin and said, "Ben has convinced me to be part of his plan that he has had for a long time. It includes the three of us. It is crazy and unbelievable, almost surreal. But Ben, you take over. You can explain it more thoroughly." Reno grabbed for another swallow from his scotch glass. Flaco looked at Ben with a very confused look as he stood up to explain his plan.

Ben went on uninterrupted for almost an hour, giving the details of his plan for the three of them to play major-league baseball again as part of the Rockies, to be together again as teammates, just as they were so many years ago. It was a possibility now because of the sports medicine and science that Ben had developed. It was Ben's dream to play again, and who better to be part of his hard work and long planning than Reno and Flaco? Reno had opened the door with his call several months ago, and now the opportunity was there to become a real possibility.

Flaco was a smart and savvy man. He was in the Hall of Fame, had a successful business, and certainly knew when he was being conned. He didn't know what to make of all this, but knew this was no con. He knew Reno was a successful man in his own right, CEO of the Rockies, and Ben always had been a serious man who didn't joke around.

"So what do you want me to do?" said Flaco. "You want me to play ball again with you guys? You want me to play for the Rockies? *No es possible*. I am an old man now, a *viejo*. *No es possible*." He stood up to pour himself another drink.

There was a several-minute silence before Reno finally spoke. "Look, Flaco, what have you got to lose in just giving this all a try? It would be all paid for by the Rockies. All you would have to commit to is the time. I know you have been thinking of getting away from the nightclub scene and getting back into baseball. This would be one way of doing it."

Ben then spoke in support. "You have the best potential of all of us to make a comeback. You have the natural ability and past experience that made you a success in past years. It only needs to be reawakened."

Flaco's expression changed from the jovial smile to a more serious look. "*Mi loco amigos*, you scare me with all this. How can it be?"

Ben moved closer to Flaco, putting his hands on his shoulders. "This can happen. Trust me, Flaco. I will need you to be in Aspen as soon as possible, and work with you through the winter. In the spring, if you don't want to continue on, we will stop. You will see results that will astound you." Reno nodded his head up and down affirmatively.

Flaco now was excited and agitated as he started talking to himself about the incredible possibility of his old friends speaking the truth. After several minutes of this, he finally sat down and looked up at Ben with disbelief.

"I can't believe I am saying this, but I trust you guys and hope this is not a dream. Okay, I'm in. Give me a few days to make some arrangements, and I will get to Aspen. I will have to buy winter clothes. I have nothing for the cold weather."

Reno and Ben laughed.

Flaco stood up and hugged each man as he nervously said, "*Los tres viejos, Dios mio!*"

Chapter 6

Flaco arrived in Aspen on Halloween. He fit right in at the airport when Ben picked him up because he was wearing a straw hat, a brightly colored pink and purple tropical shirt, and yellow Bermuda shorts with black knee-high socks, and sandals. His thick, dark sunglasses were out of place as well because Aspen was seeing its first big snowstorm of the season. Flaco had seen snow only twice before, when he was visiting family in New York for the holidays. However, this was a real winter scene.

As he was waiting with Ben for his luggage, several people complimented him on his "great costume." Ben was able to give Flaco a down parka as they loaded up the van and headed up to the institute.

"I shouldn't be surprised it is snowing in the mountains, but I wasn't prepared for this, amigo," said Flaco with a shiver.

"The surprises have only just begun, Flaco," said Ben with a smile as the van slowly headed up the narrow mountain road to the institute.

Ben and his staff wasted no time getting Flaco going. Kyle started the preliminary evaluations in the same fashion that he had with Reno. Stress testing, strength testing, neuromuscular coordination testing, full physical exam with complete blood chemistries, and orthopedic evaluations were completed in the first three days. Surprisingly, Flaco had no major red flags and passed all the testing very well for a guy in his sixties.

He also had good endurance and strength, which surprised Ben as he went over the results with Kyle. It appeared that Flaco had some very strong genes on his side.

Ben decided there was no problem for Flaco to proceed with the training, and he could start it off vigorously without too much of a delay. He did not introduce Flaco to the Simulator, Rotator, or special suits yet, wanting to proceed with at least six weeks of basic training geared to the weaknesses of his fitness.

The first sessions were with Reno and Ben. It was fun, and Flaco took to it with good spirits. At first, the basics of endurance and strength training techniques were hard for Flaco to adjust to, but with the friendly competitive banter from Reno and Ben, he took it in stride.

Flaco did have a natural ability to go longer on the treadmill and lift more weight than Ben and his team had anticipated. In just three weeks, he was able to keep up with Reno on most of the routines that Kyle had them going through.

After six weeks, Flaco was showing signs of getting bored with the repetition of the long daily workouts. This prompted Ben to become more specific and jump to the next level of training. It was time for Flaco to begin the routines that would be necessary for playing baseball at a high level again.

Flaco had just finished a three-hour jog on the treadmill using the glucose polymer drink and being infused with the endurance enzyme Ben had used at the Leadville hundred-mile trail race. He was lying down on the massage table as the masseuse started his work.

"How did those last thirty minutes feel, Flaco?" said Ben as he approached the massage table.

"*Muy bien,* Benny. It was amazing that I did not feel too tired. I could have kept going. I have not felt this good in many years, amigo. You must be giving me special steroids or something."

Ben laughed before he explained that there were no steroids or illegal, harmful substances being used. "No worries, Flaco, you do surprise me with your natural abilities. These workouts come so easy for you." Flaco acknowledged that he had noticed this in his early athletic days and assumed it was because he was just so good. "We are ready for you to begin some training that I think you will find very interesting," said Ben with a big smile.

When the masseuse was done, Flaco followed Ben into the Simulator and Rotator room for the first time. He had Flaco change into a Rockies uniform and put on cleated shoes. He gave him a choice of bats and led him over to a batting cage that had the video simulator and pitching machine. "Take a few swings as Umberto throws you a few pitches."

Flaco smiled amusedly as he took a bat and stepped up to the plate. The video showed Umberto, the Cubs' ace, starting a windup and delivering a fastball. Flaco just stood there as the ball went whizzing by.

"*Dios mio,*" he said as, one by one, each fastball flew by. Flaco was able to get a piece of a few that he fouled off, but there was no match here. He was way out of his league.

After a few minutes, Ben walked over with the computerized rubber suit. "Here, let us put this on you, and try again."

The suit fit perfectly on Flaco, but he was uncomfortable with the tubes and wires that were coming off the suit, feeding the bank of computers against the wall. He stepped in again as Umberto wound up and threw another fastball. Flaco started his swing, but after that first millisecond, the suit took over. He had no control over his swing motion as the bat came around instantly to meet the fastball head-on and connect with a shot that left Flaco light-headed and faint. He was beyond words as Ben came up.

"You all right, Flaco? You look a bit pale," said Reno with a grin.

"I must try again," said Flaco in a daze. One pitch after another, the suit initiated and coordinated Flaco's swing after reading his own inherent neurological input and then delivered the necessary motor firing pathways to connect with the ball coming from the Simulator. It truly was amazing for Flaco, and even Ben, to watch him connect with pitch after pitch within just a few minutes of wearing the suit.

Ben went on to explain how his bio-mechanist and computer expert, Louie Marlo, had programmed the videos, Simulator, and suits so that every top pitcher in both leagues was in the computer and the Simulator could duplicate each pitcher's best pitches to all parts of the plate. It could easily be seen that by using this equipment regularly, a batter could become programmed themselves. They would have the advantage of having their own musculature trained by the suit, and by a repetitive process learn from the Simulator each one of the pitchers' motions and pitches. One could practice daily, and for as long as one wanted, to face any of these top pitchers over and over again.

Ben then showed Flaco the Rotator, the swing trainer, with its variable isokinetic resistance program. It trained one to strengthen and improve the velocity of his swing. It gave the trainee power at the plate by using a very sophisticated computerized system.

Flaco was very impressed, and now excited, with the prospects that lay ahead. He saw for the first time what Ben and Reno had been talking about, and it made sense. It was science fiction, but he now saw the possibilities, and Flaco was now more than willing to follow Ben's lead.

Chapter 7

The Christmas season in Aspen was always a magical and special time. The snow-laden roofs and streets, decorations and lights, were right out of a picture postcard. The quaint shops and well-adorned lodges and hotels, the many tourists walking about in their colorful ski clothes, carrying skis over their shoulders and laughing, made the town an exciting place to be for the holidays. The slopes were loaded with snow. Powder conditions existed on all of Aspen's four ski mountains.

Ben, Reno, and Flaco had been well into their training now over the past six weeks and ready for a little break. Reno was headed back to Denver, and Flaco to Miami. Reno and Flaco had progressed very well in all aspects of their training. Reno was throwing hard and with good control, but he still had trouble with his endurance and could only last for fifty to sixty pitches.

Flaco had his timing down and was hitting the ball solidly. They both were leaner and more confident in their actions, almost to the point of being a bit vain. They were turning back the clock with Ben's help and were euphoric.

Ben figured they needed a little humility training to snap this overconfidence in their newfound athleticism.

The group was at breakfast, having their usual high carbohydrate and protein diets, and scheduled for a short workout before Reno and Flaco were to leave. It was snowing, but not hard, and there was little wind.

"Today we are going to try something a little different than our usual two-hour morning run. In one hour, we will head over to the Nordic center for your introduction to the most demanding aerobic sport there is, cross-country skiing. Wear the polypro suits you have been given, gloves, and knitted hats, and at the center, we will supply you with the necessary equipment," said Ben with authority.

Reno was suspicious but agreeable to a new change. Flaco, however, was excited and enthusiastic about the prospect of being on the snow. He had no idea what cross-country skiing entailed.

They got to the Nordic center and were introduced to Mike, the local cross-country coach. He had helped Ben learn the basics years ago and had continued to coach him in all the fine points of waxing, equipment, and techniques. Ben had become a very competitive master skier through the years and was able to stand on the podium at the national championships with a bronze medal.

Ben loved the sport. The discipline involved with the aerobic training and the techniques of classic and skate skiing took years to perfect. The aerobic demands were huge, but one could find his own pace on the snow and enjoy the quiet glide through the woods at any level of fitness or age. Ben had been involved with the US Nordic cross-country and biathlon teams for years and was director of their sports medicine program. He knew the sport at the highest level.

At the Nordic center, Mike was quick in getting the equipment ready and fitted before the group headed out to the trails. Reno and Flaco looked like a couple of elves with their tights, stocking hats, and Nordic boots on.

"Christ, I hope nobody sees me that knows me," said Reno as he gingerly walked over to Mike.

"*Linda muchacha, senor Reno,*" said Flaco, joking at their appearance in tight black tights and tight jerseys.

Flaco, however, was having a hard time staying upright, continually trying to catch his balance, slipping and sliding on the snow, complaining his boots were "*muy* slippery." The firm arch and plastic sole of the Nordic boot were strange for him. He was definitely a man out of place, but was determined that this would be a piece of cake.

Mike got them into their ski bindings and instructed them in the diagonal stride of classic technique. "It is like walking and gliding," said Mike as he gracefully danced along the track effortlessly.

Flaco made one stride before falling head over heels in the snow. "*Konuo!*" he yelled as he went flying with poles and skis in every direction. Reno was a little more coordinated in the technique and was able to move along the track slowly. Ben helped Flaco up and spent more time getting him stabilized on the skis and not fighting the fall. It took some time, but the pair eventually started to move in a smooth fashion single file down the track, following Mike and trying to mimic his technique. Ben took up the rear and was amused by the picture he saw before him: two old fairies sliding through the woods in the snow, laughing yelling and cussing as they occasionally lost their balance. They were huffing and puffing very hard to keep up with Mike, who was keeping the pace very slow.

"It's a good workout!" yelled Reno after thirty minutes of skiing, and Flaco, although humbled by it all, was starting to get into the rhythm and enjoying the new experience of gliding on top of the snow.

After sixty minutes of this, they were exhausted. Mike brought them back to the Nordic center following a much-appreciated shortcut. They were done, and their egos were deflated. They thought it should have been a lot easier after all the hard training they had been through.

"When you get back after the holidays, we will make this a regular workout. You will become real 'Nords' after all this," said Ben. "It will be a good toughening experience, as well as an excellent aerobic workout that we can do outdoors during the winter. It will keep things interesting."

They all thanked Mike as they sat around the fire at the center and had hot chocolate spiked with Ben's glucose polymer drink so they would recover fast. The three had bonded pretty well now and had come a long way. Ben was very optimistic about the prospects of success.

Chapter 8

Reno didn't take the elevator as he hiked up the thirteen flights of stairs to the executive offices of the Colorado Rockies. He was surprised at his prowess in not having to stop and not being out of breath as he entered the glass doors of the opulent offices.

"Good morning, Rita, the boss is expecting me," he said to the officious but attractive redheaded secretary.

She smiled and commented on his youthful appearance. "You seem so different, Reno, since I last saw you. Are you working out now?"

Reno smiled and acknowledged he had joined a new and special health club per doctor's orders.

"Go right on in. Mr. Cartwright is waiting for you. Can I bring you some coffee, or carrot juice, perhaps?" Rita said with a grin.

"No thanks, Rita." Reno walked through to the large office of Tobias Cartwright that was located a few steps down a white marbled corridor. "Hi, Toby" he said as he held out his hand to the large, opulent-looking man behind the desk.

Toby Cartwright remained seated as he shook Reno's hand, looking up through his thick fourteen-karat-gold-rimmed glasses. "Hey Reno, sit down and let me sign this audit report. Paperwork, paperwork, paperwork is all I seem to do around here," he said gruffly.

When he finished and looked up at Reno, his face flushed and wrinkled as his mouth tried to utter his surprise at the way he looked. "Jeez, I can't believe how different you look since I last saw you in the fall. You look fantastic, pal. What the hell have you been up to?"

Reno smiled from the large green leather chair that engulfed him and said, "It's why I am here, Toby. I want to detail the plan I have for the Rocks this season, and it has to do with my appearance. You are going to have to hear me out on this one. Just bear with me until I have given you the whole story."

Toby sat back in his chair, looked at Reno with amusement, and said a slow "Okay."

Reno got up and started pacing the large room as he unfolded the plan Ben David had proposed. He was very complete in the history of Ben's relationship with Flaco and himself in the minors. He left nothing out about the injury Ben had and the subsequent success of the medical career he had fulfilled in sports medicine. He went into the new and amazing accomplishments that he had witnessed firsthand and explained the program he and Flaco had been following for the past six months. He then outlined his thoughts about the next few months before the season started, how he wanted the team to go to Aspen before spring training and have three to four weeks with Ben and his staff. Finally, he ended with the idea of Ben, Flaco, and himself being part of the team and actually playing games in Rockies uniforms.

"It would be the greatest publicity stunt in the history of baseball. Three old former teammates in their senior years leading the club to a pennant," said Reno before he finally sat down.

Toby finally stood up and came out from behind his large mahogany desk. He went over to the bar and poured himself a whiskey, looked out the large glass windows at the Rocky Mountains, which were covered with the white winter snow, and took several minutes before he spoke.

He turned around to Reno with a deadpan expression. "You are serious, aren't you, pal?" He then approached him, stood in front of him, and looked down at the man who had the fate of the Rockies in his hands for the coming year.

"I am dead serious, Toby, and I know there are some risks, but after what I have seen and experienced, we have a damn good chance to pull this off."

Toby knew Reno very well. He respected his baseball experience and knowledge of the game. He had put him in charge with full authority to do what he felt would be necessary to get the Rockies in the play-offs. He usually was not surprised or shocked when he heard new proposals from his executives, but this time he was. He hadn't expected this from Reno, but he saw an excitement and confidence come out of him that he had never seen before.

"Reno, you have my confidence and trust, but I have to see more. Go ahead and get our team organized to follow this program from Dr. Ben, and I will meet you down in Arizona at spring training for an update and to meet him. Then I will make my final decision. You are the CEO and manager of this team, so what you say goes for now. You will have my full support until the end of spring training camp. I will make my own mind up about all of this before opening day. If you are right, this will be the biggest and craziest deal baseball, and the Rockies, has ever seen. If you are wrong, it is the end for you professionally, and it will be years before I or the Rockies live it down."

Reno again paced the room and nervously agreed with Toby's thoughts. "Great minds think alike, Toby, and I truly appreciate your confidence in my judgment about this. Bottom line will be that our fans are going to love it!"

Reno had a lot of work to do over the next few days, but the first thing he did after leaving Cartwright's office was to call Ben and tell him the go-ahead news.

"The old man is with us, so plan on the team getting up to your place in just five days. We can spend four weeks in Aspen before heading down to Arizona for spring training. Pitchers and catchers will leave early, but you and I have to stay in Aspen with the team until we all can go down to Scottsdale."

Ben was pleased with the news and thanked Reno for his support and confidence. He couldn't hold back his excitement about the prospect of playing major-league ball after all these years. It was the dream he had focused on ever since Johnny Vee gave him his walking papers in Tampa.

Chapter 9

The town of Aspen was used to celebrities, movie stars, and sport heroes who vacationed there, but the excitement was unprecedented when word got out that the Colorado Rockies were coming to town to train. There was some confusion as to why a baseball team was coming to snow country to train, especially in March, when the slopes were full of snow and the weather was cold and still wintry.

Ben had given several interviews about the sports medicine program that the institute was offering, explaining that this was a way to get an early start on the season. He explained the scientific rationale behind the pre–spring training camp, but the questions kept coming back to the notion that illegal substances or blood doping was being planned. Ben explained that the program was intended to get the players evaluated completely, from medical to physiological parameters, and use training techniques that were revolutionary in helping with endurance, neuromuscular coordination, and power.

The institute became a very busy place. Reporters and news media were always hanging around and wanting to observe and tour the facility. Ben and the staff obliged, having special meetings with the media and giving tours daily. The Simulator and Rotator were demonstrated, as well as the basic equipment used in the evaluations and training. Nutrition was discussed, and the sports drink Ben developed was explained. The news headlines in the sports pages insinuated that the Rockies were using new and secret scientific methods to make them play-off contenders, even though Ben went to great lengths to explain what they were doing. However, the enzyme converter, the bio-mechanical computerized rubber suit program, and the plans for Flaco, Reno, and Ben were not discussed.

The team members of the Rockies were a bit dubious at first, but were impressed with the fitness demonstrated by Ben, Reno, and Flaco. Their interest increased when they saw the Simulator and Rotator in action. They were fine athletes, and only a few were overweight and needed to be in better endurance shape.

Ben stressed this form of fitness for everyone, not just the pitchers. All positions were involved in the full endurance and resistance training programs to have their baselines moved up a notch. A few of the older players were not used to this vigorous training schedule and did complain, but Reno did not take any argument and insisted that this had to be done. The players stopped complaining when they saw Reno and Flaco doing the same training and, in some cases, outperforming them.

The first two weeks, the players had some minor problems adapting to the vigorous training schedules and Spartan lifestyle of the Institute, the controlled diet, and the structured exercise programs. But, by the third week, they started having a good time as their bodies started to adapt and as they shared the same challenges together as a team.

Ben was impressed with the performance of the hitters in the Rotator and Simulator. It took them little time to figure out the timing and power outputs in their swings. The special rubber computer suits were not mentioned. By the end of four weeks, all the players felt positive about the experience. Reno was extremely pleased with this beginning for the team and looked forward to Scottsdale and spring training, when the specific talents of playing baseball could be demonstrated.

Flaco, who went through all the training with the team, was a great inspiration to the younger players. He was in the Hall of Fame, and a role model for many of the players, especially the Hispanic players. It was a joy to see him interact with players during the training, laughing and joking all the time. His fitness and abilities in the Simulator and Rotator were impressive enough that several of the players asked if he was making a comeback.

Old Flaco only would smile and say, "*Muy viejo, mi amigos, no es possible.*"

The players kidded the threesome, calling them the "Tres Viejos," the "Three Old Men." A strong bond developed in the team as the training period came to an end. The Rockies players realized the benefits they had received over the past month, and were extremely interested in continuing the use of the Simulator and Rotator during the rest of the year. Reno realized he would have to arrange this somehow during the season and called a meeting with Ben.

The meeting was at the Jerome Hotel, over a fine meal in a private room. It was only Reno and Ben, as Flaco had headed back to Miami and would meet up with them in Scottsdale.

"I am happy with the way things went, but we have to have a more definitive plan as to our roles in the coming months," said Reno with his mouth filled with the first bite of filet mignon.

Ben countered with his thoughts. "Marlo has now developed the throwing and hitting suit so it can be worn without wires connected to the computer. It is now wireless and on a telemetry system that allows it to be portable. Flaco, you and I can wear the suits under our uniforms and play ball with them on with the laptop or iPhone controlled by someone in the dugout or stands. I was hoping that the suit training that we did would no longer require us to use the suits. However, to play at the level we need to play at, it is not going to be possible. We will need to use them for a time. We will also need to make the Simulator and Rotator available to all of us during the season. Marlo is working on making them more compact so they can be moved to Denver and set up at Coors Field. He should have that done by opening day. I would insist that we keep the rubberized computer suits a secret from the team, but realize we have to tell Tobias about all of this.

"Flaco, you and I can use the enzyme converter since it is not using an illegal substance, but I also insist that only the three of us use this. The team can use the glucose polymer drink with no restriction, and we can see how spring training goes before deciding on any other changes. You have to start throwing to batters right away, and we all have to be prepared for the scrutiny of the league and media about our involvement. We are going to be the examples of what strong sports medicine advances can do to improve the performance of not only baseball players, but any aging athlete who has aspirations to perform at high levels. This is our mantra, and the league or any other facility can test or examine us to their hearts content."

Reno shook his head in agreement as he looked seriously at Ben. "It's going to be quite a ride, Ben. I hope we are up for it all."

Ben smiled and dug into his steak. "I have waited for this chance for a long time, and I think we are ready to make the plunge."

They finished their meal and walked out into the cold Aspen air. "Thanks, Ben, for giving me another chance, and the same goes for Flaco. It is amazing that we can go back to those days in Geneva so long ago, when we were so young and strong. God bless the Tres Viejos," said Reno with his voice in a tearful choke as the two walked to their car.

Chapter 10

It was dry, hot, and sunny, without a cloud in the sky, as Ben got off the plane in Phoenix. Aspen still had some winter left, and the change of climate was a surprise. He was overdressed. By the time he got his luggage and rental car, he was sweating profusely, but finally got relief from the rental's air-conditioning. The drive to Scottsdale was not far, but traffic made it slow. The hotel was close to the Salt River Fields, and Ben had no trouble finding it. It was the biggest hotel in Scottsdale, on the golf course, and landscaped with colorful desert horticulture, appearing as an oasis in the vast desert sands of Arizona.

After checking in, Ben showered and changed his travel clothes for more comfortable attire, went to the hotel restaurant, and met Reno.

"A bit different than the snowy mountains of Aspen, eh, Ben? Glad you made it okay. Are you ready to go tomorrow?" said Reno, greeting him as he stood up from his private booth in the corner.

"You bet, waiting for this a long time, Reno."

The two sat down as Reno asked the waiter for a couple of beers, root beers, that is. "We are in training now, have to stay disciplined," he said with a grin.

Reno outlined the schedule for the next couple of weeks, starting with a team meeting in the morning. "After the meeting, uniforms will be fit for the newcomers, and the first practice will be in the afternoon. You and I will stick together with the pitchers and catchers, while Flaco will be with the infielders. We'll keep a low profile to start, ya know, just working out with the boys, try to gradually see how it goes."

The plan was for Ben and Reno to work together as battery mates and gradually assimilate into the whole group. They had ten days before the first exhibition game. Ben and Reno finished their dinner quickly, trying to control their excitement for tomorrow's first day of spring training.

Ben woke up early, had a light breakfast, and headed out to the Salt River Fields for his uniform fitting. He carried his glove and spikes just like a rookie reporting for work. He felt like an eighteen-year-old, forgetting he was sixty-five. His body was fit from all the years of keeping it so, and he had anticipated this second chance with total confidence. He knew the concepts of his thinking were solid, but untried in the real world of elite competition. Not only was it a personal test for him physically, but a test for his professional life and reputation. Ben had had success in the past with field testing his work, especially in the endurance fields of running and cross-country skiing, but this was the big time of major-league baseball. It was a time to prove himself and relive the chance he had missed so many years ago.

Ben was pleasantly surprised at how well the uniform he was issued fit, as well as how light it was, This was in stark contrast to the first uniform he had been given years ago in Geneva. He looked like most of the team as he entered the diamond through the dugout tunnel. The Arizona sun was bright, and the field was a beautiful green and tan.

The white chalk lines outlined the diamond with a distinct boundary.

"Hey Benny, over here," said Reno in the right field grass.

Ben had trouble recognizing him at first in his well-fitting uniform and with the sun behind him. Reno casually threw a ball at Ben, which he caught instinctively.

"C'mon, let's warm up," said Reno as the two of them lined up in the outfield for a game of catch.

There were other players warming up as well. Some pitchers were running sprints in the outfield, and others were throwing the ball back and forth with the catchers. It felt good to be throwing as Ben tossed the ball with accuracy back to Reno.

Reno smiled, reliving the days with the Geneva Redlegs, remembering this scene with Ben, as they had followed this warm-up before every game. Here they were in a major-league spring training camp getting ready for a great adventure. It was an amazing concept to accept.

They were not wearing their computerized rubber suits, saving them for a more demanding performance. They were just warming up and getting loose like all the other players on the team. The other players didn't pay much attention to them, as they were involved in their own work-outs and the practice was very short. Some took batting practice or infield practice, and most just played catch and pepper in small groups. This was the first afternoon of practice, and all knew that starting tomorrow, things would get more serious.

Early the next morning, Ben and Reno met in Reno's field office at the Salt River Field. They put on their rubber computerized rubber suits under their uniforms, and Marlo, who had made the trip, arriving the night before, was all set with the computer programs for them on his iPhone. Flaco had arrived last night as well, and now tapped on the door of the office as Ben and Reno were finishing getting dressed. Flaco was in good spirits and quite excited about putting on the uniform again. Marlo fitted his computerized suit, and Reno had his uniform for him to wear right in the office. After they all were dressed, they went out the corridor to the locker room and found their lockers, where their gear was stowed.

The locker room was filled with Rockies players, and many surprised looks found the three as they entered. "It's the Tres Viejos!" yelled a player, and the room resonated with laughter. Reno laughed as well and yelled back that they were the team's new secret weapon this year. More laughter took place before Reno raised his arms to quiet the group.

"We have been training, as you all know, at the sports medicine institute in Aspen since last fall. We are going to participate in the team's practice this spring just to help out. Flaco will be with the infielders, and Ben will be with the pitchers and catchers. I will be everywhere, but also will be with the pitchers and catchers. Let's get to business and start working hard together as a team. The sooner, the better." Reno finished his brief talk and headed out to the field, leading the Rockies with a slow jog.

Not all the infielders had reported to camp yet, but the rookies and a few of the utility fielders were there taking infield practice. Flaco joined in at shortstop, but he was having a tough time with the ground ball. He couldn't get down quick enough, and his throw for the double play was slow. It became obvious he was out of his league compared to the younger players. He took longer breaks, not because of his endurance, but because he didn't want to be embarrassed any more. Perhaps he wasn't going to be able to make the cut. His computerized suit had always been programmed for hitting, not fielding or throwing, so he was playing on his own inherent abilities at shortstop.

It didn't take long for Reno and Ben to draw the attention of the players and a few of the media who were at the practice. Reno was on the mound in the bullpen, throwing to Ben. His suit had been activated by Marlo, who was sitting in the first row of stands above the dugout. The suit and iPhone worked perfectly. Reno was firing a good moving fastball, and his slider was falling off a table, just like the old days.

Ben handled the pitches well, being very comfortable behind the plate. Soon players stopped what they were doing and watched the bullpen action that was taking place. A crowd started to develop around Reno and Ben that clapped and cheered as Reno fired one after the other into Ben's mitt. Everyone was amazed, including Reno, with his performance.

Reno stopped throwing and smiled as he yelled out to the crowd, "C'mon, get back to business! This isn't a freak show!"

The groups of players broke up and went back to their activities shaking their heads and wondering what they had just seen. The media started to gather and ask questions that Reno didn't answer.

"I'll give a press conference after practice." He went over to Flaco and told him to take throws at first base. Flaco was tall and a good target. He had no problem catching the ball even if it was in the dirt. "First base could be your new position, Flaco. Let's try it out."

Flaco agreed with a nod and trotted over to first. He handled the throws well from the other infielders, grinning as he became more comfortable with the position. He then started kidding his fellow teammates if their throws were not right on the money. Reno smiled at Ben as it became obvious this was a good choice. Flaco was like a little kid, laughing and dancing at first base as he realized this was going to work.

Ben took his place in the batting cage after most of the other team members had hit. Ben, hitting left-handed, began to connect with the ball well. The throws were straight down the middle with moderate speed, and it was no problem to get his timing down. The computer's input to the suit, initiated by Ben's swing, worked very well. Ben finished with a few vicious hits that left the ballpark on a line.

Reno and the other players had smiles of amusement at the performance. "You haven't lost much in that swing of yours, Benny," he said.

Others who were watching were very impressed. Flaco came running over to the cage, complimenting Ben on his hitting, then took his turn in the cage and started swinging. He also put on a very good demonstration of his hitting skills. He had been an excellent hitter during his playing days. Marlo had him tuned in perfectly with the computerized suit, and Flaco hit consistent line drives to the wall in left.

At the end of practice, the team was in very good spirits as they headed into the locker room. Reporters swarmed around Reno and started asking questions all at once.

"Whoa! Slow down, fellas" he said with his hands up. Reno sat down on a folding chair in the dugout and started answering questions one at a time. He explained who Ben was and how they had been teammates years ago in Geneva.

"Benny was my catcher, and with Flaco on that team, we won the league championship." He explained how Ben had gotten injured and then went into medicine, finally specializing in sports medicine, and founding the Rocky Mountain Sports Medicine Institute. "The Rockies are going to use the latest methods of sports science and sports medicine to improve our chances this year, and Dr. Ben David is going to lead this endeavor. Flaco, Ben, and I have been following a special program at the institute, and it has worked wonders. The three of us are going to try to make the team and demonstrate how these methods can make miracles happen."

The reporters immediately asked about the use of performance-enhancing drugs or other illegal methods.

"We have been using basic conditioning practices specific to baseball performance and have used training equipment to bring us up to our current level. It is like rekindling our old talents from when we were playing major-league baseball. On the field today, you have seen some of what we have already accomplished. I'll have more to explain, but right now, I have to take a shower." Reno ended the meeting, took no more questions, and headed to the showers.

The Rockies were front page the next day, and on all the major news channels. It didn't take long for the media to really ramp up. The Rockies camp was overrun with media, and the press agent for the team was overwhelmed with the continuing bombardment of questions. Ben and Reno were upset with the amount of time they had to spend updating the press agent and answering the many questions about their newfound youth and talents. It got to the point that Reno restricted the media from practice until the last twenty minutes, when the team did some stretching and cool-downs. The players were amused by it all, still not believing that the Tres Viejos were the real deal. It wasn't until the final weeks of spring training and the intramural games amongst themselves that things began to sink in.

Reno was almost un-hittable, but only for one inning before he started to get tired. Flaco hit the ball well and played first base with relative ease. He also could run the bases well with his light, skinny frame. Ben would catch Reno for the one inning he pitched and would warm up pitchers in the bullpen. The miraculous was becoming routine.

The first game of the spring training season finally arrived, and it was with the Dodgers in Scottsdale. The stands were full at least two hours before the game, and the media were in full attendance. The extreme curiosity provoked by the news of the Tres Viejos was all over Phoenix, and the crowd anticipation was at a level that had never been seen before at the Salt River Fields in Scottsdale.

When the Rockies took the field, only Flaco started, but the fans erupted in thunderous applause and cheers as he took the warm-up throws before the game.

Reno looked lean and youthful to the crowd as he met the visiting manager of the Dodgers, and the umpires, at home plate before the game started.

"Jesus, Reno, you look like you have been taking very good care of yourself, or had a body transplant," said Leo, the Dodgers manager.

"I have found a very good doctor and am eating my veggies," said Reno, laughing as he handed over the scorecard.

"Are you planning to pitch today?" said the chief umpire as he looked over the card.

"Yep," said Reno quickly.

Leo smiled in surprise and said, "This is going to be a very interesting game, boys. Can't wait to see it."

They all shook hands, and Reno started for the dugout, but could see the umps crowded together and laughing in a private conversation as he moved away.

The game started after a short delay, but it became very apparent in just a few innings that the Rockies were in better shape by the way they played. They were quicker, ran out all batted balls, and seemed to be more animated as they ran hard to reach grounders and long fly balls hit into the gaps.

Flaco was amazing with his funny antics at first. He did a little dance at the bag when he had to anticipate getting the ball from one of the infielders. He made no errors, and although he had no hits, he hit the ball hard each time. One ball he hit almost made it over the left fielder's head, but he made a phenomenal catch for the out.

The score was 4–2, Rockies. The fans loved what they were seeing and couldn't wait to see if Reno was going to pitch. He was warming up in the bullpen with Ben, getting a great deal of attention from the fans sitting above him. At the end of eight innings, it was time for the closer to come out and finish it. Reno stopped his warm-up and started out slowly to the mound to start the ninth inning.

The crowd erupted as he and Ben started to warm up before the first batter stepped in. Ben could hardly temper his emotions, realizing this was finally happening. But, he started to focus on Reno and his play, putting the noise of the crowd out of his consciousness.

Reno was nervous as well, throwing his first few throws well out of the strike zone. He finally settled down, and his last warm-up throw had very good speed.

Marlo was all set in the first-row box seats, with the iPhone, giving the thumbs-up to Reno as he looked over for reassurance. Ben threw down to second with no problem, giving him unbelievable satisfaction. The ump signaled to play ball.

The first batter for L.A. was the shortstop and leadoff hitter, Manuel Pella. He had led the league in stolen bases the last three years. He tried to suppress a smile as he stepped up to the plate. Reno went into his windup and fired a shot that was high and inside. It surprised Pella, causing him to jump back just in time to prevent getting hit. He hadn't anticipated the speed generated by the old pitcher. When he stepped back in, he was more hesitant, and the smile was gone. Reno fired two more fastballs that Pella fouled off, just getting a piece of the ball. The next pitch was a beautiful slider that fooled Pella completely. He did not swing as the ump yelled, "Strike three!"

"Damn," was all Ben heard as Pella walked back to the dugout. The next two batters were a bit more ready than Pella. They stepped in with serious looks and concentration. However, each popped up to the infield for the final two outs.

The Rockies won, and the fans stood up and cheered as Ben trotted out to the pitcher's mound to congratulate Reno. Flaco joined his former teammates, as did the rest of the infield, jumping up and down as if they had just won the World Series. All had gone well for this first test of the Tres Viejos, and they were riding high as they finally were allowed off the field by the fans and the media.

Chapter 11

Tobias Cartwright had a big smile on his ruddy face as Reno walked into his hotel room office in downtown Scottsdale. The Rockies had performed well above anyone's expectations. They had won all ten games of the preseason. Reno had pitched very well and was the closer for each win.

Flaco had no problems playing first base. His height and athletic ability made him a good target that the infielders had increasing confidence in as the preseason progressed. He also was hitting the ball well, but not as consistently as Ben. Ben had become a real threat with the bat. He never struck out, and when he hit the ball, it was a good hard connect. He also had hit four home runs. Ben's main catching duty was to go in when Reno pitched the last inning. However, he did catch a few of the other pitchers for a few innings without making an error. He was especially gratified to see his throws to second be quick and accurate, a process he thought he would never see again.

"Hey Reno, what a miracle you guys have pulled off," said Tobias as he directed Reno to a chair. "How the hell did you do it? Are your methods legal, and do I have to worry you're using illicit substances?"

Reno smiled as he sat down in a big leather chair. "No worries, Toby. The methods are state-of-the-art sports science, and Ben has developed some training methods that are revolutionary. It is like science fiction. I feel I am in a dream with the whole situation."

Tobias moved behind his big desk and lit up a Cuban cigar. He took his time, puffing smoke rings up to the ceiling before he spoke again.

"The Rockies have been on the lips of every media publication and television sports commentator for the last two weeks. The Denver fans are going nuts, and our preseason ticket sales have sold out for the first time in the history of the franchise. There is no better way to start the season. So I don't give a damn as to how you have pulled this off, as long as you aren't hiding something illegal."

Reno reassured him that nothing illegal was being done, that it was all possible because of the genius of Ben David. He briefly explained the Simulator and Rotator to Tobias, and wanted the money to get them transferred from Aspen to Coors Field so the team could use them on a regular basis. He did not mention the computerized suits that they were wearing, but did mention that Marlo from the sports medicine institute needed access to the field and locker room. He also needed a box seat ticket for every one of the Rockies' games, both home and on the road.

"No problem, Reno, I would like to see these machines in action. I will have my secretary arrange things for Mr. Marlo as well. I won't ask why he needs to be at every game, but I trust you, and I will let the matter rest for now."

Tobias was happy and excited as he ended the meeting. "Opening day is going to be something. The Tres Viejos will be the new heroes of Denver. My press agent can't wait to get the ball rolling on the publicity. Better get yourself prepared for stardom."

The two laughed as Reno left. Tobias went back to his desk and continued the slow puffs on his Cuban. He looked at the halos of smoke as they floated up to the ceiling. He knew he didn't have the whole story and wondered if Reno was correct in what he had just said or if he was holding something back. The profits were going to be huge, and the Rockies may have a chance for the play-offs if spring training was any indication of how things could go. He had to let this Dr. Ben and his methods lead the way. He hoped Reno was right.

Chapter 12

The weather in Denver was good the week before opening day at Coors Field. The team had arrived ten days before and had the good fortune to be able to practice at the ballpark twice a day in warm sunshine. Kyle Burton and Louie Marlo had managed to get the Simulator and Rotator set up at Coors in the indoor batting area. The machine and video needed some adjustments, but they got it working perfectly before the team arrived. Marlo also set up the computers for the rubberized suits and tested them with Reno, Flaco, and Ben when they were alone. They decided to use them for a short time, and do some field testing in one month to see if they still needed to use them. Ben was hoping that neuromuscular learning would have taken place by then since they would have been using them for over six months.

The team was using the Simulator regularly. The videos of the opposing pitchers had been programmed in, and it was a real advantage for the hitters to time their swings to the various pitching actions that the machine could produce. However, it became a problem due to time restraints. There was not enough time during regular daytime hours for all the team members to use the machine as long as they wanted. Nighttime usage increased, causing Reno to be concerned that sleep was being compromised.

The Rotator was also used regularly to improve the power stroke of the swing. However, it was not as popular because it felt too much like the mundane aspects of repetitive training. Ben thought that another set of machines might have to be produced, but there was not enough time or money for that right now.

Tobias Cartwright made his visit to observe the equipment in action and was quite impressed with what he saw. "Dr. David, you have produced some exciting prospects for this club, and I am grateful for this."

Ben responded that the reward, to be able to play with his old teammates and make a quasi-comeback with the Rockies, was invaluable to him.

"It is remarkable that this is happening, unbelievable actually," said Tobias when Ben and Reno had finished giving him the tour of the equipment. "Join me for lunch at my box today, and bring Flaco. I want to get to know the Tres Viejos better."

After the morning practice, the three men met at the enclosed private suite of boxes that were for the owner and his guests. They looked over the beautiful grounds of Coors Field. In the bright Colorado sun, the field appeared as a Hollywood movie set that was ready and waiting for some action. They were served lunch in a formal dining setting that was more like dinner than the lunch most were accustomed to.

Tobias joked, "Can you get me in the same shape that you are in so I can play? I am only a few years older than you guys."

They all laughed, but Ben said in a serious voice, "With enough time and with the appropriate sports medicine concepts and methods, it would be possible to consider a shot at some sport that you had an aptitude for."

Tobias looked nervous as he said with a smirk, "I was never an athlete or good at any sport." He was uncomfortable hearing Ben's statement. It seemed so impossible, yet he saw the seriousness in the statement as it was made. "You fellas are in a position to be the new heroes and role models for all the old guys who dream of the good old days. If this can be pulled off, it will make history. The Rockies fans will love us if we are successful and laugh us out of the league if we screw it up. The front office and I are behind you on this, and we will see what the league says. They will be watching us like a hawk. I expect you to tell me if there is any jeopardy in all of this."

They all gave affirmative nods and finished their big lunch, enjoying the food and the view from Tobias's box. Ben thought about the computerized rubber suits that had been kept a secret so far, but he kept quiet, following Reno's advice of "wait and see."

Chapter 13

Opening day for the Rockies was a classic spectacle. The weather was perfect. The mountains in the background had just a hint of snow on the peaks. They stood out against the robin's egg blue sky in bright sun like faraway snow castles. The field was manicured perfectly, with white chalk lines and deep green infield grass. The sold-out crowd filled the stands early to get glimpses of the highly popular Tres Viejos," whom the media had hyped so much.

Tobias was ecstatic seeing the crowd fill in the seats with so much anticipation and excitement. The Rockies were going to play their main rivals, the Chicago Cubs, and they were going to face their ace pitcher and Cy Young Award winner Umberto Gonzales. He was a twenty-game winner and owned a hundred-mile-per-hour fastball and quick-dropping slider. He was very hard to hit. The Rockies had used his video on the Simulator frequently, it being the most popular during the preseason. The team was ready for him.

Ben was nervous as he took infield practice as second-string catcher. His throws to second were sharp, and he quickly lost his nervousness as he saw how good he was throwing.

Flaco had a huge grin on his face as he received Ben's throws at first base. He yelled loudly with each of Ben's perfect throws, "*Muy bien, Bennnny!*" He was loose and confident as he did his little dance routine when he received the ball. This gave Ben a chuckle and relieved his tension.

Ben, Reno, and Flaco had on the computerized suits, and Louie Marlo had his ready position behind the Rockies dugout with his iPhone. He had figured out how to use automatic programming for the suits so he did not have to manually key in for every pitch. The suits now had their own miniature computer attached inside the fabric of the suit. Marlo was there with his iPhone, ready to act only if there was a failure with the suit.

Marlo also had been working on a recognition program that would identify which pitch was coming from a pitcher as his windup or stretch started. This data, and the video that had been logged into the computer, were extensive. However, it would be some time before it was perfected enough to use. Marlo had kept this a secret from Ben as he worked on it by himself. This was his private project.

Ben was in the bullpen, warming up the Rockies' starter, as the announcer blared out, "And here is your Colorado Rockies!" rolling off "Colorado" with several 'rrrrs'.

The Rockies took the field amongst thunderous applause, with most of the attention on Flaco, who was starting at first.

The game started off with the first Cub batter hitting a single. Flaco held him at first, but had been ready for a bunt that never came. The second batter, hitting lefty, smashed a shot that took a quick bounce in front of Flaco. Expecting the bunt, he started to hedge in toward the batter as the ball came at him like a bullet. The old instincts and reflexes fired off, and Flaco got his glove up in time to stab the ball. He had plenty of time to throw to second and recovered in enough time to dance back to first to receive the throw for the double play. It truly was a beautiful play on his part.

There was a brief silence as the crowd took a second to realize what had happened before it erupted into an explosion that rocked the stadium. The fans were going nuts with what they had just seen. It was a moment of recognition that suspended belief. Old Flaco still had what it took. The Rockies retired the side with no runs and one hit.

Umberto warmed up, looking like a giant on the mound. His six-foot-seven, two hundred-and-thirty-pound frame was intimidating to the hitters standing just sixty feet away. The first hitter was a bit anxious as two strikes were fired in without a swing. However, the next pitch, a slider, was anticipated. The batter connected, hitting a sharp single to left. Umberto, not fazed, fired up a fastball to the next batter, who tried to bunt and popped it up for an out. The third-hole hitter, their best hitter, stepped in and, with his confidence from the Simulator, pulled the ball down the right field line for a double, driving in a run. The next four hitters all hit the ball well for singles. The Cubs were in a state of shock, and Umberto was getting agitated and very angry.

Flaco stepped in as the number eight hitter. The bases were loaded. Umberto yelled at him in Spanish that he was going down. Flaco wasn't sure if that meant he was going to be dusted or struck out. Flaco, who was used to these situations, wasn't intimidated, and just smiled at the big pitcher.

Umberto took a full windup rather than throwing from the stretch. He would not accept the fact that an old man could hit his powerful fastball. He threw it high and inside, dusting Flaco back. The crowd erupted into a frenzy of boos and catcalls. The ump gave a warning that Umberto ignored. He wound up again, letting Flaco know his heater was coming. Flaco was ready. Again, the Simulator had him locked in, and Marlo had his rubber suit activated.

The ball flew off of Flaco's bat, into the left field stands for a home run. Flaco took his victory lap around the bases with the crowd in unimagined pandemonium. He did not look over at Umberto, knowing that the pitcher would take any excuse for a fight. The Cubs' manager came out and, after a brief conference with his game-winning pitcher, took him out before the first inning was over. Umberto walked off the field humiliated for the first time in his career. He kept looking at Flaco in disbelief and shaking his head as he walked to the dugout. The Rockies were leading seven to nothing, and it was only the first inning.

The new pitchers for the Cubs were not in the Simulator's video memory, so the Rockies hitters faced new blood. The game then progressed uneventfully. By the time the eighth inning came around, the score was Rockies ten, Cubs three.

Reno came out of the bullpen and warmed up to pitch the last inning. Ben was to catch Reno, taking over behind the plate. He couldn't believe he was finally in a big-league game, catching his old mate Reno against the Cubs. This was the impossible achievement he had dreamed about all these years.

The crowd acknowledged the old-timers with thunderous applause and cheers. Reno went right to work, throwing fastballs to the first two hitters. The ball moved well as the computer did its job coordinating Reno's neuromuscular function to perfection. Each hitter was able to hit the ball, but not out of the infield. The third batter stepped in and hit a double, quieting the crowd for a few seconds. The crowd had been in a constant chant of "Rockies, Rockies" and on their feet since Reno took the mound.

Ben noticed that the runner on second was not very attentive to play, taking a big lead off second and not getting back to the bag very quickly after each pitch. The last thing the runner expected would be a pickoff attempt by an old and rookie catcher in the last inning. Ben had given Reno and his second baseman the pitchout and pickoff sign for the next pitch. Reno threw the pitchout, and Ben fired a strike to second, picking off the runner, who was late getting back by several feet. The throw was beautiful and right on a line. It was retribution for those last embarrassing days in Tampa when Ben couldn't even throw to the pitcher accurately.

Reno and Flaco knew how much this meant to Ben, and they jumped up and down, hugging him at home plate. The Rockies won, and the crowd remained, cheering Tres Viejos for twenty minutes nonstop after the game was over.

The Rockies locker room was mania and confusion. There were media people everywhere asking the three old players all the usual questions as to how it felt to play in their first game after all these years and to play so well. Ben gave the usual mundane answers, while Flaco played it to the max, dramatizing his home run blow by blow.

Reno finally had the locker room cleared and addressed the team. "We all played well today, and it was a momentous game for us old guys. Ben has made it possible for age to be less of a factor if one can work hard and take advantage of science. We, as a team, have benefited from his programs, and we now have a good start. It is a long season, but let's maintain the momentum and keep working hard as a team."

The players all gave a loud "Yes!" in unison as Reno finished his pep talk.

Reno, Flaco, and Ben went into Reno's private office to get out of their suits before heading for the showers. "You did it, Benny boy," said Reno with a big grin. "I never have had so much pleasure playing baseball, especially being able to share this with you two."

Flaco just laughed, while Ben just smiled and gave the two a big hug, not saying anything. It was truly an amazing day for baseball, and truly an amazing achievement for sports medicine.

Chapter 14

All of Colorado was now aware of the Tres Viejos. Reno, Flaco, and Ben were the subject of conversations across the state and the nation. People wanted to know much more about them and how they were able to get themselves into such wonderful physical condition to play for the Rockies. Of course, there were skeptics who insisted that some illegal or harmful procedures were being used. There were calls for medical examinations, blood tests, and even birth certificate verifications.

Reno, along with the Rockies management and Tobias Cartwright, played their cards close to their chests. They did not admit anything was illegal and gave out no specific information other than the pat answer that they followed new, hard training techniques that had rekindled their own inherent talent for playing baseball.

The Simulator and Rotator, along with the sports drink, were the only techniques explained. Other teams in the league, of course, were very interested and wanted to know more, but time was not on their side, and no one else had the expertise that Ben David and his staff in Aspen had.

As the season went on, the Rockies continued to play excellent baseball, winning the majority of their games at the time of the All-Star break in July. Reno continued to pitch no more than the last two innings, and was leading the league in saves. He had found his old form, but could not sustain it for more than the two innings, even if his pitch counts stayed below forty.

Flaco also started to show fatigue and had to sit out for a few games each week. The season was too long for him to play on a regular basis. When he did play, he played well, hitting .345 with twenty homers at the break.

Ben, however, could play more regularly since he was in the best shape. He began to catch more than just the innings Reno pitched. He even started several games, playing about half the games on the schedule. He got better as the season progressed and devoted the time to keeping up his general conditioning programs that he'd followed for the past forty years.

The team used the Simulator and Rotator on a regular basis, which had its video bank kept up to date by Marlo. Now, all of the starting pitchers, and 75 percent of the relief pitchers, were programmed in. Marlo also completed the video recognition program that could discern which pitch the pitcher was going to throw by the way the computer would analyze the beginning movements of the pitcher's windup. He had managed to develop a device that the batter wore in his helmet that would beep one, two, three, or four beeps, telling what the pitch was going to be.

This information, he knew, was very controversial and probably would not be accepted by the team or the league. But science was science, and he felt an obligation to develop methods that would improve performance for athletes in safe ways. The powers other than himself would have to rule on them.

Reno was the only Viejo picked for the All-Star Game, as one of the closing relief pitchers. He was privately ecstatic since he never had been picked when he played in his earlier years. Ben and Flaco, who traveled to Saint Louis with him for the game, fully supported him. Tobias had a party for the team during the break and had Reno as the guest of honor. The Denver Chamber of Commerce had a confetti parade for him downtown the day before, and he was on the cover of every senior citizen publication in the country, captioned with the heading of "It can be done!"

Reno lived up to his billing and pitched shutout innings for the National League as they won by three runs. It was a bit problematic since he had to get into his computer suit privately. He did this in his hotel room and reported to Busch Stadium in his uniform. After the game, he had to leave the field in his uniform, which roused the suspicions of the National League officials. His only explanation when asked was he liked his privacy, being very abrupt with the answer.

When the season began again after the All-Star break, the Rockies were in first place in their division by six games. The Phillies had the best record in the National League, but the talk was that the Rockies finally had a chance for the play-offs, and even the league championship. Some even mentioned the world championship. Attendance was at its maximum at every game, both home and away, and Tobias, in the front office, was beyond ecstatic.

The team continued to play good baseball, and the "Tres Viejos" were constantly hounded by the fans and media. Offers to appear on TV were a daily occurrence, with only Flaco taking advantage of all the attention. Reno did some public relations work at the insistence of the front office, but Ben tried to avoid it as much as he could.

Ben was still responsible for the workings of the Rocky Mountain Sports Medicine Institute and tried to get back to Aspen whenever the team was home in Denver. He had left Kyle Burton in charge with extra staff, and Marlo was always being called by other major-league teams to inquire about the Simulator and Rotator. He constantly had to put them off, but related that their interest was much appreciated. Marlo also had to add staff to get the videos of as many pitchers in the league as possible. He then had to do the correlations with the bio-mechanical computers and download all the information so the pitch could be recognized before it was thrown.

Marlo worked on this eighteen hours a day. He even had the the video recognition of the opposing managers downloaded so he could predict their signs from the dugout. His assistants made trips to all the National League fields with their small video cameras to record this information. Marlo did all of this on his own, without Ben knowing any of it. He did know that Marlo had talked about these possibilities, but the applications and specifics had not been discussed. Marlo knew he had to have a long meeting with Ben to discuss all the possibilities of his work. The financial and performance impacts of all of this were quite obvious and significant.

Chapter 15

The second half of the season went by very quickly. The Rockies, as a team, were playing the best baseball in the league. There was not a doubt that they would be in the play-offs. This was a reality by the time September rolled around.

The team relied less and less on the "Tres Viejos" as the caliber of the team play continued to improve. Reno still was the closer if the game was tight, but he also did a great job as manager, knowing his players and their abilities well. He was savvy as to when to hit and run, steal, pinch hit, and take his pitcher out. He also knew when he himself had to be kept out of the game if he didn't have his good stuff..

The season ended with the Rockies in first place in their division, which was no surprise. They were due to face the Philadelphia Phillies for the National League pennant.

The fans in Colorado were crazy with so much enthusiasm for their Rocks, that every game was like a World Series win. Coors Field vibrated with the noise during the home games, and the sports bars were crowded, selling more beer than ever when the team was on the road. Tickets were at a premium, not being available except for very high prices. Potential league championship and world championship tickets were sold out far in advance. Everyone was ready to see the Rockies take the pennant.

The Rockies didn't disappoint. It was a close series, but the Rockies pulled it off by outhitting the Phillies and their strong pitching staff. Reno held them off in the sixth game to end the series and give the Rockies the National League pennant.

Flaco and Ben did not contribute much and played very little. They were not needed because of the Rockies' excellent performance in all aspects of the game. Flaco would play a few innings when they were at home, and gave the fans a good show with his comedic antics at first, and his occasional strong performance at the plate.

Ben played only when Reno went in to pitch the closing innings and showed he could handle himself well behind the plate. He didn't hit as strongly as the first-string catcher for the Rocks, but seemed to hold his own very well, getting a few singles and one extra base hit that sealed the sixth game for the now National League champs.

In Denver, the excitement for the Rockies was huge. Another parade downtown was larger than the previous one that had been held earlier. The Tres Viejos were still getting a lot of attention, but it was much less than usual because the fans realized what a great team they had in the Rockies.

The regular players started to acquire hero status themselves, which pleased Reno, Flaco, and Ben very much. They were part of a great team, just like they had been so many years ago in Geneva. This, however, was the big time, and under quite different circumstances. It was like a dream for all of them, but now the reality of the World Series was next.

Chapter 16

Louie Marlo was ready to meet with Ben about his new findings. The programs were ready, and the equipment had been perfected so every batter with the new beeping helmet would know the pitch before the pitcher released the ball. Also, it was easy to create a program that would identify the signs of opposing managers signaling their players to bunt, steal, hit and run, and which pitch to throw. It was an awesome advantage to have.

Marlo had arranged for Ben and Reno to come to Aspen for a demonstration of the programs, insisting on not revealing his secrets before they could arrive at the sports medicine institute. He had everything arranged in the conference room for his demonstration as Ben and Reno arrived on an early flight.

"You sure have my curiosity up, Louie, with all this secrecy," said Ben as he looked around the room at the equipment Marlo had set up.

"Sit down, Ben, and you too, Reno. I want to show you what I have come up with."

Reno and Ben sat down and focused on the screen as Marlo went into his explanations. When he was finished, Ben had a very serious look. He tried to curb his surprise and uneasiness by rubbing Rosie, the big Newfie, who had sat down next to him. Rosie missed him at the institute and wouldn't stay away when she saw him arrive.

"This is amazing work, Louie. You truly are a wizard. But your genius will put baseball back rather than forward. How can it be ethically right to have this technology when other teams don't have it?"

In some ways, it was a rhetorical question that Reno picked up on immediately. "You science boys are opening up issues that are beyond the scope of improving performance. This isn't kosher in my book." Reno was pale and sat down next to Ben and Rosie.

Marlo went on about the techniques of the Simulator, Rotator, the energy drink, and enzyme converter, all were new techniques that helped athletes perform better. The golden rule was always, if it was safe, effective, and legal, then no restrictions applied to the science of improving an athlete's performance. Science could not be held back. The legal and moral issues had to be determined by the governing bodies.

It is a well-known precedent that when new innovations become available, they are criticized by those who don't have them. He gave the examples of the biking technologies that only the pro racers had access to. New bike innovations were used only by the company pros, who would use them until they became more widely known. Biking companies would always keep quiet some of the secrets that were developed for the pros, even if the company would say the models for the public were the same.

The cross-country ski technique of skating was banned until the European and Scandinavian teams were up to speed on the technique. New designs of skis, bases, and waxes were kept secret by the nations that developed them, who still kept the secrets of some of their waxing formulas for themselves. Aerodynamic helmets, golfing equipment, race car engine improvements and body garments were guarded by the commercial companies with high degrees of secrecy. The list went on and on.

Ben knew what Marlo was talking about, especially as it related to his own motivations for going into sports medicine. The inadequacies of the treatment for his throwing injury that ruined his career during his prime was a good example of why it was so important to keep moving the science forward.

"Do we draw the line and forget about the science involved?" said Marlo as he sat down with a frustrated expression.

Ben did not hesitate in responding. "The new information you have presented is in a realm that creates too great an advantage. It is a form of cheating. It is different when we present information for improving sports performance that is safe and effective, but we are restrained by the rules of the sport and competition. We can't use these concepts now. We are stretching the rules keeping the computerized suits a secret. In fact, I think we have to tell Tobias and the Rockies front office about them as soon as possible. We have to then go to the commissioner with all this so he is informed as well."

Reno, who was now agitated, agreed. "I knew this day was coming, but couldn't accept it. Denial was my rationalization, especially in light of all the fun we were having and the team playing such good baseball. I'll set up the meeting right away with Tobias."

Ben watched sadly as Marlo shrugged his shoulders and walked away.

Chapter 17

Tobias was in a great mood when Reno and Ben were shown into his office. "Welcome, gents, what's up?"

Reno wasted no time on trivialities and started out by going into the facts of the computerized suits they had been wearing. Ben took over and began to go into the physiology of it all, trying to belay the anguish that had begun to spread across the previously cheerful face of the owner.

Tobias finally was able to respond with a soft but angry voice. "This is preposterous. I have never heard of such fantasy."

Ben continued on and also explained the new techniques Marlo had presented the day before.

"We have to tell all this to the commissioner," said Reno when Ben finally finished.

"This will ruin the Rockies. Our fans will never understand," said Tobias as he got up and began to pace the room, reiterating, "This will ruin us. This will ruin us." He looked at Reno with utter helplessness. "How could you do this to me? How could you do this to baseball?"

Reno said he would submit his resignation immediately and tried to find the useless words of apology.

"Your resignation is the last thing I want to see. That would escalate the whole damn situation. I agree we have to tell the commissioner and put ourselves at his mercy. We will fly to New York tonight." Tobias buzzed his secretary and instructed her in making the necessary arrangements. He impressed upon her that this was urgent.

Chapter 18

Reginald Schubert had been in baseball for thirty-six years. He had been the commissioner for the last twenty-five. He loved the game and would do anything in his power to protect the national pastime. He would even bend the truth if necessary to accomplish this, but, when backed against the wall with an issue, he wouldn't compromise himself. He did what was right. This was very apparent when he minimized the collateral damage that could have occurred to baseball during the steroid catastrophe.

He was curious about the urgency of Tobias's request to meet and didn't allow Tobias, Reno, Falco, and Ben to wait long as he ushered them into his large, wood-paneled office.

"Welcome, Tobias, and great to see you again, Flaco, and you too, Reno. You must be Dr. David. Can I call you Ben? I am happy to finally meet the Tres Viejos that have done so much for baseball this season."

"Call me Ben, sir," said Ben as the four were led to a conference room adjacent to the commissioner's office.

"We have a serious dilemma, Reggie," said Tobias in a stern voice. "I am going to let Dr. David explain the situation since it deals with him the most."

Ben stood up and carefully began to explain the approaches he had taken early on to get the Rockies' performance improved through the science of sports medicine. He went into the extensive fitness training, nutrition concepts, and finally the equipment he and his staff had developed for baseball.

"I am fully aware, Ben, of the Simulator and the Rotator," Reggie interrupted.

Ben was not surprised, since most of baseball was aware of these items. Then he started to explain the computerized suits that Flaco, Reno, and he were using. Reggie's expression changed to a more serious frown as Ben went on to explain them in detail.

"I want to make it clear that only the three of us knew about them, and we never allowed anyone else on the team to use them. It has been our secret. Mr. Cartwright was informed of all this only yesterday."

Reggie had a look of astonishment as he asked Ben to repeat the unbelievable description of these amazing suits. "This is science fiction. How in the world did this happen?" he said with agitation. He finally took in his disbelief as Ben continued on with his explanation. Reggie stayed silent for a few minutes, contemplating the impact that this would have on how baseball was going to be played from now on. He then looked over at Reno with a penetrating look. "What did you think when you used the suit and pitched those innings this season?"

Reno stood up and answered in a straightforward tone, "I thought of it as an amazing scientific achievement. It was as if I went back in time. I was captivated by the mystery of it all. I did train long and hard, putting myself in Ben's hands, and was totally amazed at the results. My body became strong and young again. It was too hard to pass up as time went on. I did not initially believe that it would have led me and the team to where we are now. The more I played and saw what our team was doing, the more I wanted it to go on. The team began to play extremely well following the example us old guys were giving them. I soon observed, as the season went on, that winning was more dependent on the team play than it was on the three of us. The experience was too amazing and gratifying. It became impossible to consider stopping."

Tobias nervously added that the Colorado fans were in a state of frenzy. "We won the pennant, and we're ready to play in the World Series. There would be a riot in Colorado if this were made known and the Rockies were not allowed to play for the world title." He went on to say that baseball was, in reality, the eventual winner due to the success of the Rockies and its players. The interest in the game had reached heights it had never seen in recent times. Senior citizens had seen what results three old men could achieve, and it gave them, and everyone else, new hope that age was not a limiting factor as once thought. The impossible was possible.

"Did you think you were doing anything wrong?" Reggie asked in a soft voice.

Flaco spoke up first. "No, it was fun, and we were old men having a good time helping our team."

Ben then explained how science was advancing faster in areas that would make it difficult for governing boards to determine what was wrong or right. "Look at how the International Olympic Committee changed the rules allowing professional athletes to finally compete in the Olympics. The rules of the old guard had to change as new information became available."

Ben then became very serious and gave the recent information that Marlo had proposed on the pitching prediction computer that could tell the batter the pitch before it left the pitcher's hand. He also explained the ability to recognize opposing managers' signs to their players that gave orders to bunt, steal, or hit and run.

Reggie was shocked at the realization that this could potentially become a reality. "Did you ever use these devices this season?" he asked with a serious frown.

"No, we have not," said Ben quickly. "This was crossing the line, making it more like cheating. What we did was only to improve our abilities, abilities that most assumed were over the hill a long time ago. It gave old folks a vision that age was not always a factor in athletic performance. We did not take an unfair advantage that could be considered illegal by the current rules of baseball. It was a training technique that enhanced our own inherent ability and talent."

Reggie stood up. "I have heard that one before! I will have to think about all this and get some of my consultants on board. This is going to be a major decision for me and for baseball. It has major consequences. It has to be made quickly with the World Series championship only two days away. Be in my office tomorrow at seven a.m. sharp. This will be difficult, but I will have a decision tomorrow."

The four left the office somberly, with Tobias in near tears at the possibility that the Rockies would be ruined and his reputation and career would be over.

Reno, Ben, and Flaco went to the hotel bar to talk this over. "I don't care what the decision is, *amigos*. We were not the reason the team is in the World Series. The players are *muy bien* and worked hard to get to this point. We helped, sure, but the team would be here without us. They would be playing for the title even if we never played. I had fun, and it was a miracle that we could play together again after all these years. You did it, Benny boy. You are a genius. You did nothing wrong, and you made me and Reno very happy." He raised his beer glass. "To the Tres Viejos."

Ben and Reno laughed and clinked their glasses with his. "The Tres Viejos!" they all shouted together.

Chapter 19

Reggie looked very tired as he led Tobias, Reno, Flaco, and Ben into his office early the next morning. "I have been up all night trying to make the right decision, and have come to a conclusion. This could go many ways. It could be complete elimination from the championship for the Rockies and banishment for all of you from baseball, with heavy fines to the organization. Maybe even fraud charges. Or, it could be kept completely secret without anyone knowing what occurred. This would be intolerable to me, as would the former. I have made a decision somewhere in the middle.

"First, the suits must not be used by you again. You will remain on the team and play, but without the suits. You will have to play with your own abilities and not give any suspicion to the fans by suddenly not playing. They expect you to play. It will be very amusing for me to see how you accomplish this, or what explanations you give for not play-ing up to your previous levels. Eventually, the technology of these suits can be revealed, but only at the appropriate time and place. You did take advantage by using them for your own personal gain. However, I do feel that your play did not contribute in a significant way to the Rockies winning the division. The team played well without you, especially in the second half of the season, and probably would have won the division anyway. You did contribute, I believe, to the mental aspects that drove your team's success, but that cannot be measured objectively.

"This type of technology should be shared and made available by presentations at scientific meetings before it is used by a major-league baseball team. I do realize, however, that competitive sport has a hard time ignoring methods that give a team or player an edge.

"Secondly, you must not allow the technology of predicting a pitcher's pitch to the batter or stealing signs from opposing managers to become a reality. This is cheating, and I appreciate your candor and commitment to the game by not accepting or using these techniques. I realize that governing boards have to develop ways of dealing with the incredible advancements that are being made today in sports medicine. I intend to form a consulting staff of sports medicine experts to advise me and keep me up to date on these advancements. We have to be prepared to deal with these issues before they become detrimental. I know that there are many examples where this technology can make the sport safer and help athletes maximize their performances in safe and dramatic ways. We as governors have to make the rules in accordance with these advances so fairness can be maintained. It is a new and great challenge for me and for baseball, a challenge that is necessary to pursue and achieve.

"Finally, the three of you will retire from baseball after the season is over. You should start to think of an explanation and plan that will be acceptable to your fans and to baseball. I will want to review this plan before it becomes public. Reno can continue to manage, but his playing days are over. I expect you, Dr. David, to continue your sports medicine pursuits and hope that we can work together in the future, with you heading my panel of experts to keep us educated in these matters.

"If any of these parameters are not met, then I will come at all of you, and the Rockies, with everything at my disposal to make the public aware of your actions this season. Baseball and the fans of baseball will be painfully hurt by this exposure. I count on you to make sure this doesn't happen. You have helped baseball by stimulating the intense interest in your achievements, and by getting the enthusiasm back into the game. Seniors have found new hopes in your examples, and my office has now been made aware of the new responsibility we have in learning more about what science has in store for us in the future."

Tobias sputtered with supercilious thank yous to Reggie for saving the Rockies and his reputation. They were not going to be ruined. Reno and Flaco also thanked the commissioner for his understanding and fair decision. Ben, who was the calmest, was impressed with the commissioner's Solomon-like wisdom in dealing with the issue. It was a well-thought-out decision that had baseball's best interests in mind.

"I have great respect for your wisdom and leadership. I look forward to helping you and your office in the future. It will be a pleasure to work with you," said Ben as he gave his hand for a very sincere handshake.

The commissioner smiled. "I will be very interested in watching the three of you as you finish this season. It will be quite enlightening to see the Tres Viejos in a different light now that I have all the facts. Good luck, Doctor."

Chapter 20

The first game of the World Series was to take place in New York. The Yankee's were the American League champions, winning the pennant by defeating the Chicago White Sox in four straight games. The Yankee's were in first place the entire second half of the season, being ahead of the second- place team in their division by ten games. They were strong in every aspect of the game, They had the top players because they could pay the top salaries in baseball. The Yankee's were the overwhelming favorite to win the series over the Rockies.

Reno was nervous about pitching without the computerized suit. There wasn't much time between their meeting with the commissioner and the start of the first game of the World Series. Ben and Reno had spent hours in the bullpen the last twenty-four hours, throwing and trying to see what the results would be without the suits. Reno definitely had lost speed and accuracy, but he still had great movement on his slider.

Ben realized that he felt uncomfortable, again trying to "think" his throws without wearing the suit. This was the same problem he had when he had injured his arm and lost his natural coordination. Ben had thrown without the suits before and done okay due to his high level of fitness, but there was noticeable improvement and security with the suit. This was now the World Series, and with the pressure, it brought back all the mental images of his premature downfall so many years ago. It made Ben very nervous.

"We have got to realize that we can do this, Reno. The suits have conditioned our musculature, so we can expect no major differences without them. We have been living, sleeping, and playing baseball for about a year. This situation is more mental than physical. We have done the time to be as good as we can be. It is only a matter of proving to ourselves that our bodies have the ability to play at this level."

Reno smiled as he continued to throw pitches. "I hope you're right, Ben. Otherwise, we are going to be the biggest clowns baseball has ever seen."

The Tres Viejos were not scheduled to start the first game of the series in New York. There was obvious disappointment since they were so popular with the media, having so many interviews and stories published about their appearance in the World Series. Reno was treated as a superstar in the media, and the fans of New York would not let him rest whenever he appeared in public.

Before the first pitch of the first game, Reno was bombarded with catcalls and jeers by the Yankee fans.

"There is no chance in hell for an old man like you against the Yankees!"

"You're not in the boondocks anymore! This is New York!"

"You're a fluke! Judgment day is here and now, Gramps!"

Reno tried to ignore all this, but his insecurity kept him on edge. The New York manager calmed him a little when they met at home plate for the exchange of scorecards before the game.

"You're my idol, Reno. Didn't think you guys could pull this off. It is a miracle that you are playing against us in the World Series. My hat's off to you, buddy."

Reno joked a bit about taking his Geritol and vitamins, but thanked him for the kind words. He was nervous, and the group at home plate recognized his uneasiness.

"Good luck, gentlemen. Let's make this a hell of a series," said the home plate umpire, then stepped back and yelled, "Play ball!"

The first game was all Yankees as they took command of the game from the first inning. Stanley Jones, their ace pitcher, started and was in top form. He had the best record in baseball, using his hundred-mile-per-hour fastball and several off-speed pitches that kept the best batters off-balance and guessing. The Rockies only managed two hits in the seven-to-nothing shutout. The Tres Viejos did not play since the game was so one-sided.

The second game was closer. The Rockies played good defense and managed to get three runs, but the Yankees still dominated by hitting for nine runs and the win. Flaco played as a designated hitter and, without the suit, went 0 for four. He struck out twice and grounded to the opposite side of the infield twice, swinging late behind the ball each time.

The third game was different. The Rockies exploded with seven runs, and their defense was excellent. The Yanks managed three runs and couldn't make up the deficit as the Rockies won the third game. The series was two games to one as the teams headed to Denver for the next round. The Rockies showed they could beat the great Yankees by scoring runs and playing strong defense. The Tres Viejos remained quiet.

Chapter 21

Coors field was decked out with red, white, and blue bunting that circled the stands all the way to the upper deck. A first World Series for the city of Denver and the Rockies. The city ramped up as high as their logo and trademark of; "The Mile High City." The Colorado fans welcomed the New York Yankees with the usual boos for the city slickers, but most of the enthusiasm was not against the Yankees, but adulation for their beloved Rockies and the Tres Viejos.

The stands went crazy when the pre-game introductions were made and Flaco, Ben, and Reno stood forward. The ovation didn't die down until the PA announcer finally had to ask them to stop.

Flaco started at first, while the rest of the young Rockies team hustled out to their positions on defense. The Rockies were flawless, except for Flaco. He played well at first base, but couldn't get his bat around fast enough to do any damage at the plate. The game finally ended up with the Rockies winning by six runs. It was a joy for the partisan crowd, and the chanting and cheering didn't stop until several hours after the game. The series was now tied two games to two. There were two more games to play in Colorado before going back to New York. The Rockies could end it all at home by winning them.

The next game again had the Rockies explode with six runs in the first inning. The Yankees were in a state of shock as the Rockies continued to dominate them on offense and defense. Remarkable outfield catches that saved extra base hits, and fast, error-free infield play kept the Yankees form scoring no more than three runs. Flaco again did not produce at the bat, and Reno took him out in the fifth inning. Ben did not play, and Reno did not pitch. As long as the Rockies played winning ball, Reno was happy to keep himself and Ben out of the game. The Rockies could end it all tomorrow by winning game six, the best four out of seven.

In game six, the Yankees seemed to become more serious and machinelike in their play. Jones was on the mound again and took control once more. He shut out the Rockies 3–0 and allowed only one hit. It was looking as if a no-hitter and perfect game was going to happen, but the Rockies left fielder managed a bloop single in the eighth inning, spoiling the perfect game. Reno thought about putting himself in for the beginning of the ninth, but his pitcher retired the side without a threat. The Rockies were unable to score in the bottom of the ninth, and Jones went on to win with a spectacular pitching performance. The series was now tie, three games to three, as the series went back to New York for the final game. New York had home field advantage, and predictions again favored the Yankees to win it all.

Millions around the world watched game seven in Yankee Stadium, breaking every TV record for a World Series. The stadium was more than filled, with fans standing like sardines in the bleachers. The anticipation was comparable to what one could imagine in the days of ancient Rome and the Colosseum.

The game started close and remained close for seven innings. The Rockies continued to play good conservative baseball, and the Yankees stayed right with them, collecting four runs to the Rockies' three. Flaco was the designated hitter again and finally hit the ball with more force, but got no hits, as his drives were right at the fielders. In the eighth, the Rockies scored one run to tie the score. However, the Yankees came up in the bottom of the eighth and scored two. The Rockies had only one more chance in the top of the ninth, or the game and series were over.

The New York fans could taste the victory as the ninth inning started. All were on their feet as the Rockies came up to hit. The first two Rockies hit singles, easing some of the anticipation by the crowd. The Rockies bench was now animated and excited, as they now had two on and nobody out.

The Yankees manager had Stanley Jones warming up in the bullpen along with his closer and another starter. The three had gotten themselves ready for the beginning of the ninth in case the Rockies threatened. Jones had little rest, but he needed to pitch only half an inning. Now that the Rockies had runners on first and second, the Yankees manager wasted no time in going to the mound and pulling his pitcher. He waved for Stan Jones to come in and finish this thing. It was the bottom of the Rockies' order, and he knew Reno would have to put in a pinch hitter if Jones could get out the next two batters. He pulled his ace card and put his faith in Jones.

Jones had not lost his form, as he quickly struck out the next two Rockies. Two outs, men on first and second, and the Yankees ahead by two runs. The pitcher was due up.

Reno did not hesitate. He knew that the best chance he had was Ben David. Even though Ben hadn't played in a World Series game yet, Reno had the instinct that Ben was the best choice he had on his bench to get a hit and keep it going. "Grab a bat and make yourself a hero, Ben. I know you can get a piece of the ball and keep us in there. If you can get on, we have a chance with the top of our order coming up."

Ben looked at his old teammate with a surprised yet excited look that reflected his fear. He slowly took his bat and walked out to the batter's box. The PA announcer actually announced him as one of the Tres Viejos, Ben David. The crowd went nuts at the announcement, calling out every old man cliché in the book. Stanley Jones did not change his expression, looking very serious and determined on the mound. Ben took his warm-up swings and stepped into the box. He knew he didn't have his suit on and only hoped he could get a piece of the ball and not strike out.

The noise of the crowd escalated as Jones wound up and threw a fastball strike that moved more than any pitch Ben had ever seen, even on the Simulator. The next two pitches were breaking balls that were just out of the strike zone. Ben relaxed a bit more, expecting that the next pitch was going to be a fastball. He started to have a feeling that he had experienced before, years ago during his successful days as a young player. It was that instinctive zone of knowing success. His vision became clearer, and his body became poised and ready for the next pitch. There was a sense of confidence that came over him as he concentrated on Jones and his windup.

Jones put everything he had into the next fastball. Ben called on those inner reactions and movements that he had been born with. He started his swing with every cell in his torso lining up and delivering. His body counted on this inherent ability and the ability that had been developed by the strict training it had gone through. The swing was fast and true, hitting the ball directly on the sweet spot. Ben had that old instinctive, feeling, knowing it was a good hit the instant the ball hit the bat.

Reginald Schubert was watching the game with Tobias and the Yankees' owner in the private owner's box. He was disappointed that Reno, Flaco, and Dr. David had not played as much as he would have liked during the series. When Ben stepped up to pinch hit in this critical situation, his interest suddenly peaked, and he could not hold back his amusement and curiosity. He became very excited to see what would happen next. He thought Reno and Ben must have a lot of guts to do it this way when all was on the line. He was on the edge of his chair, just like everyone else in the stadium. He watched with a nervous smile as Ben swung at the two-and-one pitch, not expecting any contact to be made. But he jumped up and screamed like a young boy as the ball was hit and went zooming over the right field wall. It was a booming home run. No doubt about the distance or the force that the ball had. He cheered with Tobias as he watched this "young old man" round the bases as if this was a normal, routine occurrence.

The Rockies bench erupted, as did the crowd. Reno and Flaco were the first ones at home plate to welcome the new hero. The Rockies jumped up and down and threw their hats in the air as if they had won the game.

"You did it, Bennny!" yelled Flaco. Reno had never shown more emotion in his life as he hugged and jumped at home plate.

The umpires were quick to restore order, as the game was not over, and the Yankees still had their half of the ninth inning to make a comeback. The Yankees crowd quickly quieted down, and an eerie silence fell over the playing field. They realized that their Yankees could lose the World Series. Stan Jones lost his usual demeanor of confidence as he took seven pitches to finally get the last Rockie out.

Reno did not have the time to adequately warm up before he made the decision to pitch the last of the ninth. Ben's performance had given him the confidence to put his reputation and his team's destiny in his hands. He had the chance to make his comeback the most remarkable in the history of baseball. Now, it was all on him, and he had to do it by himself, without the help of the miracle machines of the Rocky Mountain Sports Medicine Institute.

Ben was going to catch this last inning, but with new confidence in his abilities. He did not think twice about having a concern when he had to throw the ball. That mental obstacle was finally over. As he put on the "tools of ignorance," his shin guards and chest protector, he told Reno, "You are ready to do this, Reno. Your fastball will be the setup pitch for your slider. Waste the fastball on the corners, and come in tight and low with the slider." He gave Reno a big smile as the two of them headed out to the field together.

Reno took a lot of time warming up since he hadn't had any bullpen action after Ben's home run. Finally, the home plate umpire yelled, "Play ball!" stopping Reno's warm-up. Ben threw the ball down to second with the same velocity and accuracy as he had when wearing the suit.

Up in the owner's box, Reginald Schubert thought, *Maybe the boys are playing with the suits.*

Reno took his time on the mound. He could feel the nervousness trying to build and break through his attempt to keep it out of his consciousness. He threw four straight balls, walking the first Yankee. The crowd responded with loud clapping and stomping of their feet that rocked Yankee Stadium.

The next batter successfully sacrifice bunted, moving the tying runner to second. There was now one out. Reno tried to move his pitches around more with the next hitter. He was feeling more comfortable with his slider, barely missing the strike zone. He eventually walked the next batter, now putting runners on first and second. The Yankees' third- and fourth-place hitters were now due up. Reno realized the third-place hitter was their best, so he continued to call for sliders and ran the count to three and two. The next pitch was hit firmly toward the hole in center, but the Rockies second baseman made a diving save and threw in time to get the runner forced at second. Two outs, and runners on first and third.

The big cleanup hitter for the Yankees stepped up for his chance to be a hero. The tension in the stadium was enormous and could be felt by all, especially by Reno and the big Yankee hitter at the plate. Ben could see the tension in the batter's muscles as he readied himself for the pitch. Reno threw a fastball, with not much on it, to the outside corner. The ball was hit with great power, flying over the right field wall by several feet, but foul. The groan from the crowd was loud at the near miss. The next two pitches were fastballs well away and called balls. Reno was holding back his slider for the last pitch, so he threw another fastball inside that was again hit solidly, but foul. The sound the ball made hitting the bat caused the crowd to immediately come to their feet and yell, only to suddenly quiet themselves and sit down.

Reno now had to throw the best slider of his life. This was always his best pitch, and he had to put it in a place that the hitter would not have solid contact. He saw Ben give the sign and nod his head up and down, relaying his confidence to Reno.

The pitch came off the delivery as smooth as Reno had ever thrown. It felt very right to him as he completed his windup and came through on his wide-arc throw. He looked in this moment of time like he had when he was winning games in Geneva. The hitter, poised and ready, recognized the pitch coming in belt high, but as he swung his full swing, the ball dropped, and the bat only found air.

"Strike three!" It was over.

The Rockies won the World Series, and the Tres Viejos accomplished the impossible. They all performed as heroes and didn't disappoint themselves, or their team. They did it with their own talents, and of course, with the help of some extraordinary sports science. In the end, however, it was truly always up to them.

When the Rockies finally made it to the locker room, Reginald was waiting for the Tres Viejos as champagne flew everywhere. Reno saw him immediately and knew what he was thinking by the look on his face. He wasted no time in pulling off his shirts to expose his bare chest and the absence of the computerized suit. They looked at each other with subtle grins in recognition that the rules had been followed. The commissioner gave old Reno an out-of-character hug as the two of them were engulfed in the shower of champagne.

Flaco and Ben quickly joined them amidst the chaos and took off their shirts, showing their bare chests and no suits. Tobias was yelling and screaming while spastically trying to shake a champagne bottle and spray them all with the bubbly liquid. The five of them were the only ones who knew what had truly taken place: the great performance by the Rockies, and the unbelievable performances by three old men who had done the impossible. Reginald Schubert, the long-standing patriarch of baseball, had just witnessed the most amazing baseball performance in his lifetime, and he couldn't tell anyone about it.

Epilogue

Ben approached the big hill on the Owl Creek Trail, using the new ski binding he had developed to keep his ski tips from digging in as he put his weight forward to maximize his leverage for the V1 stride he would have to do to get up the steep grade. He could feel his skis glide smoothly, with less effort, during the climb. It had worked like a charm. This would help cross-country skiers from driving their ski edges into the snow, impeding their glide and progress when going uphill.

The snow-covered landscape kept the world very quiet along the trail, and Ben felt at peace. Things had finally settled down after the World Series. The Rocky Mountain Sports Medicine Institute had become world famous. Ben and the institute had been bombarded by media, athletes, coaches, and owners to learn more about what they did and how their secrets could be obtained by the rest of the world. It became a financial bonanza since every major-league team wanted to have a Simulator and Rotator for their teams to train with. Ben chuckled at the prospect of the world knowing about the computerized rubber suits and how much they would be worth. There were definite applications for these suits in other sports, and Ben wasn't going to stop research on them even though he had promised not to use them in baseball. He planned to publish several papers and knew that the philosophy of sport was going to face major challenges in deciding what the rules would allow.

There would always be controversy when a new ergogenic aid came along. The altitude bags and chambers that improved aerobic endurance performance were a good example of one of the newer methods being used. The techniques of using altitude training had stimulated a great deal of research until it was worked out how to best utilize the technology.

Financial availability was also a major problem. Some teams and countries couldn't afford the costs for the new technology, so performance was related to money rather than talent. This was a familiar dilemma in sports performance.

Ben was on a flat portion of the trail now and could bring his heart rate and respirations down to more comfortable levels. He cruised along effortlessly in the beautiful mountain landscape, not wanting to be anywhere else on the planet.

Flaco had returned to Miami and opened up two new bistros. His newfound fame made his business flourish, and he loved the South Beach action and lifestyle. Reno stayed on in the Rockies front office, becoming Tobias's general manager. He did not return to the ball diamond again. He continued to keep a close eye on Ben's institute, always looking for new ways his Rockies could use science to improve their performance.

Ben was also involved with the commissioner's sports medicine panel for baseball, and headed the committee. There was much to do.

The Tres Viejos had experienced the best baseball could offer, and they were thankful for it all. Reno, Flaco, and Ben saw much more of each other now. They would always have the bond of close friendship that was shared so early, and again so late, in their lives. They had achieved the dreams that were rooted in those early playing days, when they played with so much youthful confidence.

Ben David had finally finished the unfinished business that had plagued him all these years. It was a great sense of satisfaction, and he was thankful that he had been given a most unusual opportunity for this second chance.

Louie Marlo had not stayed with the institute. He left without any explanation. His letter of resignation was short and direct. Ben suspected he would pursue his innovative computerized bio-mechanical technology, and hopefully would do so ethically. Ben knew, however, that he had not heard the last from Marlo.

Ben was now approaching the ski lodge to end this good ski. He felt the pleasant, invigorating, healthful sensation that extended exercise always brought to him. He knew he was considered old, but he felt like a young man and was thankful for the way his body responded to the hard exercise. He had several new projects in the works with the US Nordic team. He had to get them done soon. He looked forward to these new challenges and was glad that his life had settled back into the more mundane routine of his work. He took his skis off and headed into the warmth and comfort of the lodge.

About The Author

Dr. Barry Mink, board certified in sports medicine and internal medicine, has practiced in Aspen, Colorado, for over thirty-six years. He is a fellow of both the American Board of Internal Medicine and the American College of Sports Medicine. He was the chief medical officer for biathlon at the 1980 Lake Placid Winter Olympics and team physician for the US Olympic team at the 1994 Lillehammer Winter Olympics. He is a Masters cross-country skier and runner, and did play professional baseball for the Cincinnati Reds after high school. He lives with his wife Peggy in Aspen, and has three daughters and four grandchildren.

Made in the USA
Charleston, SC
09 July 2012